Welcome to February's fabulous collection of books
from Harlequin Presents!

Be sure not to miss the final installment of the brilliant
series THE ROYAL HOUSE OF NIROLI. Will the beautiful
island of Niroli finally be able to crown the true
heir to the throne? Find out in *A Royal Bride at the
Sheikh's Command* by favorite author Penny Jordan!
Plus, continuing her trilogy about three passionate and
brooding men, THE RICH, THE RUTHLESS AND THE
REALLY HANDSOME, Lynne Graham brings you
The Greek Tycoon's Defiant Bride, where Leonidas is
determined to take the mother of his son as his wife!

Also this month…can a billionaire ever change his
bad-boy ways? Discover the answer in Miranda Lee's
The Guardian's Forbidden Mistress! Susan Stephens
brings you *Bought: One Island, One Bride*, where a
Greek tycoon seduces a feisty beauty, then buys her
body and soul. In *The Sicilian's Virgin Bride* by
Sarah Morgan, Rocco Castellani tracks down his
estranged wife—and will finally claim his virgin bride!
In *Expecting His Love-Child*, Carol Marinelli tells the
story of Millie, who is hiding a secret—she's pregnant
with Levander's baby! In *The Billionaire's Marriage
Mission* by Helen Brooks, it looks like wealthy Travis
Black won't get what he wants for once—or will he?
Finally, new author Christina Hollis brings you an
innocent virgin who must give herself to an Italian
tycoon for one night of unsurpassable passion,
in her brilliant debut novel *One Night in his Bed*.
Happy reading!

Dear Reader,

Hi there. Would you believe I have been writing romances for twenty-five years? Amazing! Not that I was published all that time. My first book didn't appear till 1990. You have no idea how excited I was to finally become an author for Harlequin. They are great publishers who continue to deliver quality romances for you to read.

I hope you enjoy my latest story, *The Guardian's Forbidden Mistress,* which is mostly set in Sydney. My hero is a former bad boy—a popular theme of mine. And my heroine is a darling. This fast-paced, very sexy story has a deeply emotional core, and a highly dramatic ending on a tropical island. May it leave you breathless!

Happy reading!

Miranda Lee

Miranda Lee

THE GUARDIAN'S FORBIDDEN MISTRESS

QUEENS of ROMANCE

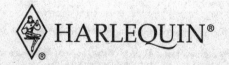

HARLEQUIN®

TORONTO • NEW YORK • LONDON
AMSTERDAM • PARIS • SYDNEY • HAMBURG
STOCKHOLM • ATHENS • TOKYO • MILAN • MADRID
PRAGUE • WARSAW • BUDAPEST • AUCKLAND

ISBN-13: 978-0-373-23465-3
ISBN-10:   0-373-23465-1

THE GUARDIAN'S FORBIDDEN MISTRESS

First North American Publication 2008.

Copyright © 2008 by Miranda Lee.

www.eHarlequin.com

Printed in U.S.A.

All about the author...
Miranda Lee

MIRANDA LEE was born in Port Macquarie, a popular seaside town on the mid-north coast of New South Wales, Australia. Her father was a country schoolteacher and brilliant sportsman. Her mother was a talented dressmaker.

After leaving her convent school, Miranda briefly studied the cello before moving to Sydney, where she embraced the emerging world of computers. Her career as a programmer ended after she married, had three daughters and bought a small acreage in a semirural community.

Miranda attempted greyhound training, as well as horse and goat breeding, but was left dissatisfied. She yearned to find a creative career from which she could earn money. When her sister suggested writing romances, it seemed like a good idea. She could do it at home, and it might even be fun!

It took a decade of trial and error before her first romance, *After the Affair,* was accepted and published. At that time, Miranda, her husband and her three daughters had moved back to the central coast, where they could enjoy the sun and the surf lifestyle once again.

Numerous successful stories followed, each embodying Miranda's trademark style: fast-paced and sexy rhythms; passionate, real-life characters; and enduring, memorable story lines. She has one credo when writing romances: Don't bore the reader! Millions of fans worldwide agree she never does.

CHAPTER ONE

SEVEN years later…

A frown formed on Sarah's forehead as she watched Derek turn from the crowded bar and slowly make his way back to their table, a full champagne glass in each hand.

In the time it had taken him to be served, she'd begun to worry about having accepted his invitation for a Christmas drink.

Sarah comforted herself with the thought that in the six months Derek had been her personal trainer, he'd never made a pass, or crossed the line in any way, shape or form.

But there was a definite twinkle in his eye as he handed her a glass, then sat down with his.

'This is very nice of you,' she said carefully.

Sarah's heart sank when he beamed back at her.

'I *am* nice,' he said. 'And no, I'm not coming on to you.'

'I didn't think you were,' she lied before taking a relieved sip of the bubbly.

'Yes, you did.'

'Well…'

Derek laughed. 'This is just a little celebratory drink. One you deserve after all your hard work. But do be careful over the Christmas break. I don't want you coming back to me at the end of January in the same shape you were in six months ago.'

Sarah pulled a face at the memory. 'Trust me. I won't ever let that happen again.'

'Never say never.'

Sarah shook her head as she put down her glass. 'I've done a lot of thinking while you've been working my blubbery butt off these past few months, and I've finally come to terms with the reason behind my comfort-eating.'

'So what's his name?' Derek asked.

'Who?'

'The reason behind your comfort-eating.'

Sarah smiled. 'You're a very intuitive man.'

Derek shrugged. 'Only to be expected. Gay men are very *simpatico* to matters of the heart.'

Sarah almost spilled her wine.

'You didn't suspect at all, did you?'

Sarah stared across the table at him. 'Heavens, no!'

'I dislike guys who advertise their sexual preference by being obvious, or overly camp. Other gays sometimes guess, and the odd girl or two.'

'Really?' Even now that she knew the truth, Sarah couldn't detect anything obviously gay in Derek. Neither could any of the women who worked out at the gym, if the talk in the female locker room was anything to go by. Most of the girls thought him a hunk.

Whilst Sarah conceded Derek was attractive—he had nice blue eyes, a great body and a marvellous tan—she'd never been attracted to fair-haired men.

'So now that you know I'm not making a beeline for you,' Derek went on, 'how about answering my earlier question? Or do you want to keep your love life a secret?'

Sarah had to laugh. 'I don't have a love life.'

'What, none at all?'

'Not this last year.' She'd had boyfriends in the past. Both at university and beyond. But things always ended badly, once she took them home to meet Nick.

Next to Nick, her current boyfriend always came across as lacklustre by comparison. Time after time, Sarah would become brutally aware that she wanted Nick more than she ever did other men. Nick also had the knack of making comments that forced her to question whether her boyfriend was interested in her or her future inheritance.

Yet Sarah didn't imagine for one moment that Nick undermined her relationships for any personal reasons. That would mean he cared who she went out with. Which he obviously didn't. Nick had made it brutally obvious since becoming her guardian that he found the job a tiresome one, only to be tolerated because of his affection for and gratitude to her father.

Oh, he went through the motions of looking after her welfare, but right from the beginning he'd used every opportunity to shuffle her off onto other people.

The first Christmas after she'd left school, he'd sent her on an extended overseas holiday with a girlfriend and her family. Then he'd organised for her to live on campus during her years at university, where she'd specialised in early-childhood teaching. When she'd graduated and gained a position at a primary school out in the western suburbs of Sydney, he'd encouraged her to rent a small unit near the school, saying it would take her far too long to drive to Parramatta from Point Piper every day.

Admittedly this was true, and so she had done as he suggested. But Sarah had always believed Nick's motive had been to get her out of the house as much as possible, so that he was free to do whatever he liked whenever he liked. Having her in a bedroom two doors down the hallway from his was no doubt rather restricting.

A well-known man-about-town, Nick ate women for breakfast and spat them out with a speed which was breathtaking. Every time Sarah went home he had a different girl-friend installed on his arm, and in his bed, each one more beautiful and slimmer than the next.

Sarah hated seeing him with them.

Last year Sarah had restricted her home visits to Easter and Christmas, plus the winter school break, during which Nick had been away, skiing. This year she hadn't been home since Easter, and Nick hadn't com-plained, readily accepting her many and varied excuses. When she finally went home on Christmas Eve tomorrow, it would be nearly nine months since she'd seen Nick in the flesh.

And since he'd seen her.

The thought made her heart flutter wildly in her chest.

What a fool you are, Sarah, she castigated herself. Nothing will change. Nothing will ever change. Don't you know that by now?

Time to face the bitter truth. Time to stop hoping for a miracle.

'His name his Nick Coleman,' she said matter-of-factly. 'He's been my legal guardian since I was sixteen, and I've had a mad crush on him since I was eight.' She refused to call it love. How could she be in love with a man like Nick? He might have made a financial success of his life in the years since they'd first met, but he'd also become cold-blooded and a callous womaniser.

Sometimes Sarah wondered if she'd imagined the kindnesses he'd shown her when she was a child.

'Did you say eight?' Derek asked.

'Yes. He came to work for my father as his chauffeur on my eighth birthday.'

'His chauffeur!'

'It's a long story. But it wasn't Nick who started my eating binge,' she confessed. 'It was his girlfriend.' The one who was there draped all over him last Christmas, a drop-dead gorgeous, super-slender supermodel who'd make any female feel inadequate.

A depressed Sarah had eaten seconds at Christmas lunch, then had gone back for thirds. Food, she'd swiftly found, made her feel temporarily better.

By Easter—her next visit home—she'd gained ten kilos. Nick had simply stared at her. Probably in shock. But his new girl-friend—a stunning-looking but equally skinny actress this time—hadn't remained silent, making a sarcastic crack about the growing obesity problem in Australia, which had resulted in Sarah gaining another five kilos by the end of May.

When she'd seen the class photo of herself, she'd taken stock and sought out Derek's help.

Now here she was, with her hour-glass shape possessing not one skerrick of flab and her self-esteem firmly back in place.

'Amend that to two girlfriends,' Sarah added, then went on to fill in some more details of her relationship with her guardian, plus the circumstances which had led up to her coming to the gym.

'Amazing,' Derek said when she stopped at last.

'What's amazing? That I got so fat?'

'You were never fat, Sarah. Just a few kilos overweight. And lacking in tone. No, I meant about your being an heiress. You don't act like a rich bitch at all.'

'That's because I'm not. Not till I turn

twenty-five, anyway. My father made sure in his will that I won't get a dime till I reach what he called a mature age. For years I had my educational and basic living expenses paid for, but once I could earn my own living I had to support myself, or starve. I was a bit put out at first, but I finally saw the sense of his stand. Handouts don't do anyone any good.'

'That depends. So this Nick fellow lives in your family home, rent-free?'

'Well, yes… My father's will said he could.'

'Till you turn twenty-five.'

'Yes.'

'When, exactly, does that happen?'

'What? Oh, next February. The second.'

'At which point you're going to turf that blood-sucking leech out of your home and tell him you don't want to see his sorry behind ever again!'

Sarah blinked, then laughed. 'You've got it all wrong, Derek. Nick doesn't need free rent. He has plenty of money of his own. He could easily buy his own mansion, if he wanted to.' In actual fact, he'd offered to buy hers. But she'd refused.

Sarah knew the house was way too big for a single girl, but it was the only connection she still had to her parents, and she simply could not bear to part with it.

'How come this Nick guy is so flush?' Derek asked. 'You said he was your father's chauffeur.'

'*Was* being the operative word. My dad took him under his wing and showed him how to make money, both on the stock market and in the business world. Nick was very lucky to have a man like my father as his mentor.' Sarah considered telling Derek about Nick's good fortune with *Outback Bride* but decided not to. Perhaps because it made Nick look as though he hadn't become successful in his own right. Which he had. 'Have you ever been to Happy Island on a holiday?' she said instead.

'No. But I know about it.'

'Nick borrowed money and bought Happy Island when it was going for a song. He personally supervised the remodelling of its largely derelict resort, built an airport on it, then sold the whole shebang to an inter-national equity company for a fortune.'

'Lucky man.'

'Dad always said luck begins and ends with hard work. He also advised Nick that he'd never become rich working for someone else.' Which was why Nick had set up his own movie production company a couple of years back. He'd already had some success but nothing yet to rival *Outback Bride*.

'Your dad's right there,' Derek said. 'I hated it when I had a boss. That's why I started up my own gym.'

'You own The New You?'

Derek gave her a startled look. 'Don't tell me you didn't know that either.'

'No.'

He smiled, showing flashing white teeth. 'Talk about tunnel vision.'

'Sorry,' Sarah apologised. 'I can be like that. I'm a bit of a loner, if you haven't noticed,' she added with a wry smile. 'I don't make friends easily. Guess it comes from being an only child.'

'I'm an only child too,' he confessed.

'Which makes my being gay especially hard on my parents. No grandkids to look forward to. I only told them a couple of years ago when Mum's pressuring me to get married got a bit much. Dad hasn't talked to me since,' Derek added, the muscles in his neck stiffening.

'That's sad,' Sarah said. 'What about your mum?'

'She rings me. But won't let me come home, not even for Christmas.'

'Oh, dear. Maybe they'll come round in time.'

'Maybe. But I'm not holding my breath. Dad is a very proud and stubborn man. Once he says something, he won't back down on it. But back to you, sweetie. You're simply crazy about this Nick fellow, aren't you?'

Sarah's heart lurched. 'Crazy describes my feelings for Nick very well. When I'm around him, I just can't stop wanting him. But he doesn't want me back. And he never will. It's time I accepted that.'

'But surely not till you've had one last crack at him.'

'What?'

'You haven't been working your butt off because some anorexic model said you were fat, sweetie. It's Nick you're out to impress, and attract.'

Sarah didn't want to openly admit it. But of course Derek was right. She'd do anything to have Nick look at her with desire. Just once.

No, not once. *Again.* Because she was pretty sure she'd spotted desire in his eyes one Christmas, when she'd been sixteen and she'd come down to the pool wearing an itsy-bitsy bikini that she'd bought with Nick in mind.

But maybe she'd imagined it. Maybe she was just desperate to believe he'd fancied her a little that day, despite his actions to the contrary. Teenage girls were prone to flights of fantasy, as were twenty-four-year-olds, she thought ruefully. Which was why she'd spent all week buying the kind of summer wardrobe that would stir an octogenarian's hormones.

The trouble was Nick wasn't an octogenarian. He was only thirty-six, and he kept his male hormones well and truly catered to. Sarah already knew that the actress girlfriend had gone by the board, replaced by an advertising executive with a penchant for power-dressing.

Sarah might not have been home personally for several months, but she rang home every week to talk to Flora, who always gave her a full update on Nick's comings and goings before passing the call over to Nick. If he was home, that was. Often he was out, being a social animal with a wide range of friends. Or contacts, as he preferred to call them.

'I presume you spend the Christmas holidays back at home?' Derek asked, cutting into her thoughts.

'Yes,' she said with a sigh. 'I usually go home as soon as school breaks up. But I haven't this year. Still, I'll have to make an appearance tomorrow. I always decorate the Christmas tree. If I don't do it, it doesn't get done. Then I help Flora prepare things for the following day. The lunch is partially catered for, but Flora likes to cook some hot food as well. Flora is the housekeeper,' she added when she saw Derek frown at the name. 'She's been with the family for forever.'

'I have to confess I couldn't see your Nick with a girlfriend named Flora.'

'You'd be right there. Nick's girlfriends always have names like Jasmine, or Sapphire, or Chloe.' That was what the latest one was called: Chloe.

'Not only that,' Sarah went on waspishly, 'they never help. They always just swan downstairs at the last minute, with their fingernails perfect and their minuscule appetites on hold. It gets my goat when they sit there, sipping mineral water whilst they eat absolutely nothing.'

'Mmm,' Derek said.

Sarah pulled a face at him. 'I suppose you think I'm going to get all upset and make a pig of myself again.'

'It's highly possible, by the sounds of things. But what I was actually thinking was that you need someone by your side at this Christmas lunch. A boyfriend of your own.'

'Huh! I've brought boyfriends to Christmas lunch before,' Sarah informed Derek drily. 'In no time, Nick makes them look like fools, or fortune-hunters.'

'And maybe they were. But possibly they were too young, and totally overawed by the occasion. What you need is someone older, someone with looks and style, someone successful and sophisticated who won't be fazed by anything your playboy guardian says and does. Someone, in short, who's going to make the object of your desire sit up and take notice. Of you.'

'I like the idea, Derek. In theory. But even with my improved looks, I don't think I'm going to be able to snaffle up the type of boyfriend you've just described at this late stage. Christmas is two days away.'

'In that case let me help you out. Because I know just such an individual who doesn't have anywhere to go on Christmas Day and would be happy to come to your aid.'

'You *do*? Who?'

'You're looking at him.'

Sarah blinked, then laughed. 'You have to be kidding. How can *you* be my boyfriend, Derek? You're gay!'

'You didn't know that till I told you,' he

reminded her. 'Your Nick won't know it, either, especially if I'm introduced as your boyfriend. People believe what they're told, on the whole.'

Sarah stared at Derek. He was right. Why would Nick—or anyone else at lunch—suspect that Derek was gay? He didn't look it. Or act it.

'So what do you think?' Derek said with a wicked gleam in his eyes. 'Trust me when I say that nothing stimulates a man's interest in a woman as well as another man's undivided attention in her.'

Sarah still hesitated.

'What are you afraid of?' Derek demanded to know. 'Success?'

'Absolutely not!'

'Then what have you got to lose?'

Nothing at all, Sarah realised with a sudden rush of adrenalin. At the very least she would not feel alone, as she often did at Christmas, especially during that dreaded lunch.

This year she would not only be looking her best, but she would also have a very good-looking man by her side.

'All right,' Sarah said, a quiver of unexpected excitement rippling down her spine. 'You're on.'

CHAPTER TWO

SARAH'S positive attitude towards Christmas lasted till she pulled her white car into the driveway the following morning and saw Nick's bright red sporty number parked outside the garages.

'Darn it,' she muttered as she pressed the remote to open the electronic gates.

She'd presumed Nick would be out playing golf, as he always did every Saturday, come rain, hail or shine. Come Christmas Eve as well!

If she'd imagined for one moment that Nick would be home, she'd have put on one of her sexy new sun-dresses this morning— probably the black and white halter-necked one that showed off her slender shoulders and nicely toned arms. Instead, she was sporting a pair of faded jeans and a striped yellow tank-top. Suitable clothes in which to decorate a Christmas tree. But not to impress a man, especially one who had a penchant for women who always looked as if they'd just stepped out of a beauty salon.

Still, with a bit of luck, she might be able to sneak up to her bedroom and make some changes before running into Nick. The house was, after all, huge.

Built in the 1920s by a wealthy mining family, Goldmine had been renovated and revamped many times since then. Its original stone walls were now cement-rendered white, with arched windows and lots of balconies, which gave it a distinctly Mediterranean look.

Because of the sloping site, the house looked double-storeyed from the road, but there was another, lower level at the back where the architecture incorporated a lot of glass to take advantage of the home's harbourside position.

Actually, there weren't many rooms in the house that didn't look out over Sydney Harbour, the view extending across the water to the bridge and the opera house in the distance. On the upper floor, all the bedrooms had individual balconies with water views, the master bedroom opening out onto a walled balcony that was big enough to accommodate an outdoor table-setting.

The enormous back terrace had the best vantage point, however, which was why it was always the place for Christmas lunch. Long trestle-style tables would be brought in, shade provided by huge canvas blinds put up for the day. Only once in Sarah's memory, when the temperature soared to forty degrees, had the lunch been held inside, in the family room, the only room large enough to accommodate the number of guests who swamped Goldmine every Christmas Day from midday onwards.

The tradition had been started by Sarah's father and mother soon after they'd bought the house nearly thirty years ago, a tradition her father continued after her mother's death, and which Nick seemed happy to honour in the years he'd been living there.

Of course, the cynic in Sarah appreciated

that Christmas lunch at Goldmine was more of a business lunch these days than a gathering of family and long-term friends. Most of the guests at the table would be the people Nick did business with, valuable contacts whose priorities were where the next few million were coming from.

Sarah was under no illusion that Nick was any different from the types he mixed with. He liked money as much—possibly more—than they did.

This last thought reminded Sarah of what Derek had implied over drinks last night: that Nick was taking advantage of his position as her guardian to live, rent-free, in her harbourside home. Although she'd defended Nick in this regard, Sarah had to concede that living in Goldmine was a huge social advantage. Not so much because of its size—some of the neighbours' homes were obscenely large—but because of its position. There was no doubt that having such an address had benefited Nick no end in the business stakes. Which was why he wanted to buy the place.

The gates finally open, Sarah drove

through and parked next to Nick's car. She frowned over at it, still perplexed that he hadn't gone to golf today.

Thinking about golf, however, reminded her of the Christmas present she'd bought him. It was a set of miniature golf clubs, with the club heads made in silver, the shafts in ebony and the bag crafted in the most beautiful red leather. She'd bought it on eBay and it had cost several hundred dollars, more than she usually spent on him.

The moment she'd seen it, she'd known Nick would like it.

But would he think it odd that she'd bought him something so expensive?

She hoped not.

Sarah grimaced when she realised he might think it even odder that she hadn't bought her new 'boyfriend' anything at all. Which she hadn't. She and Derek had discussed when he was to arrive tomorrow and what to wear, but they hadn't thought of presents.

Sarah sighed, her confidence about this subterfuge beginning to drop.

Not that it mattered all that much. She

couldn't seriously expect to achieve the miracle of having Nick suddenly look at her and be carried away on a wave of uncontrollable desire. Why should that happen now, after all these years? It wasn't as though she hadn't dolled herself up for him before. She had. With absolutely no results at all.

The truth was she obviously wasn't his type. Even with her normally lush curves pared down to the bone, she'd never look or act like the kind of girlfriend Nick inevitably chose and obviously preferred: not only super-slim, but also super-chic and super-sophisticated.

A kindergarten teacher just didn't cut it with Nick, even with a future fortune attached. If anything, that she was her father's heiress was probably a turn-off for him. Nick would not like any reminders that he wasn't entirely a self-made man. Or the fact that she'd known him when he was a nobody.

With every new girlfriend, Nick came with a clean slate.

Sarah had no doubt he hadn't told this

latest girl, Chloe, that he'd ever been in jail. Or that his ward's father had been a very generous benefactor. She felt sure Nick always represented her father these days as a long-term friend, thereby explaining his guardianship of her.

Sarah accepted these brutally honest thoughts with a mixture of emotions. There was disappointment, yes. But also a measure of relief. Because it made her realise that to harbour hopes of attracting Nick this Christmas was a case of desperation and delusion. It wasn't going to happen.

Whilst this realisation brought a pang of emotional pain—no one liked to have their longest and fondest dream dashed—the acceptance of reality also began to unravel the tight knots in her stomach. What she was wearing today no longer mattered. She could relax now and act naturally with Nick, which she would not have done with her previous pathetic agenda.

Sarah might have called Derek right then and there and cancelled his coming tomorrow, if she hadn't already told Flora when she rang last night that there'd be an added guest for Christmas lunch; her new boyfriend, Derek. Although Nick had been out at the time, Sarah had no doubt that Flora would have told Nick this news at breakfast this morning. Flora was a dear lady, but inclined to gossip.

No, there was nothing for it but to go through with this charade now.

'You'll probably be glad, come tomorrow,' Sarah told herself as she climbed out of the car and walked round to open the hatchback. Nick's new girlfriend sounded like a right bitch, if Flora's character assessment was to be believed. When Sarah asked what she was like, Flora had said she was up herself, big time.

'Just as good-looking as the last one,' Flora had added, 'but more intelligent. And doesn't she know it! Still, she won't last any longer than the others. Six months is tops for our Nick. After that, it's out with the old and in with the new. If that boy ever settles down, I'll eat my hat.'

Sarah pulled a face as she lifted her two bags out of the boot.

She would, too.

Nick was definitely not a marrying man; never had been and never would be. He wasn't into romance, either. Catering to his sexual needs was the name of his game where women were concerned.

Once Nick got bored with his latest game-partner, she was out.

He'd once admitted to Sarah when she'd been about twelve—they'd just watched a very sweet romance on TV together—that he could never fall in love the way the characters had in that movie. He'd confessed rather grimly that he didn't have any idea what that kind of love felt like.

Sarah presumed his inability to emotionally connect with women had something to do with his loveless upbringing, a subject she'd overheard being discussed by her parents not long before her mother died. Apparently, Nick had suffered terribly at the hands of a drunken and abusive father, running away to live on the streets of Sydney when he'd been only thirteen. After that, he'd been reduced to doing some pretty dreadful things just to survive.

Sarah never did find out exactly how dreadful, but she could guess.

Just after turning eighteen, Nick had finally been arrested—for stealing cars—and had been sentenced to two years in jail.

It was during this term that he'd finally been shown some kindness, and given some practical help. By a man who'd spotted his natural intelligence, a man who, for years, had generously given up many hours of his time to help those less fortunate.

Nick was put into a special education programme for inmates that this man had funded, and became one of their most successful graduates, achieving his higher-school certificate in record time.

That man had been her father.

'Sarah!'

Sarah almost jumped out of her skin at her name being called.

But when she saw who it was, she smiled.

'Hi there, Jim. You're looking well.' Flora's husband had to be over sixty by now. But he was one of those wirily built men who aged well and always moved with a spritely step.

'Got a lot of luggage there, missie,' he said, joining her behind her car and staring down at her two very large bags. 'Home for good, are you?'

'Not yet, Jim. Did you get me a good tree?'

'Yep. A beauty. Set it up in the usual spot in the family room. I put the boxes of decorations next to it. And I've hung up the lights out the back.'

'Great. Thanks, Jim.'

Jim nodded. He wasn't one for chit-chat, unlike his wife.

Jim was happiest when he was working with his hands. He loved keeping the extensive grounds at Goldmine spick and span, not such a difficult job after her father had come home from a visit to Tokyo a decade ago and had all the more traditional flower beds and lawns ripped out and replaced with Japanese-style gardens. Now there were lots of rocks and gravel pathways, combined with ponds and water features, all shown to advantage by interesting trees and plants.

Jim hadn't been too thrilled at first with the lack of grass and flowers, but he'd grown to appreciate the garden's unique beauty and serenity.

Jim picked up Sarah's bags without her asking and started heading along the curved path towards the front porch, putting paid to her earlier plan to sneak in unnoticed through the garages.

To be honest, Sarah still wished she looked better for Nick's first sight of her. It would have been rewarding to see the surprised look on his face.

Sighing, she grabbed her carry-all from the passenger seat, locked the car and hurried after Jim, who by then had dropped her bags by the front door and rung the doorbell.

'I do have keys,' she said, and was fishing through her bag in search of them when the door was wrenched open.

Not by Flora—but by Nick.

If ever Sarah was glad she was wearing sunglasses it was at that moment.

Not because of Nick's reaction to her, but because of her reaction to him.

She'd been so caught up with worrying about her own appearance that she'd forgotten just how devastatingly attractive she found him, especially when he was wearing as little as he was wearing today: just board shorts and a sleeveless white surf top, the colour highlighting his beautifully bronzed skin.

Sarah's thankfully hidden gaze travelled hungrily down his body then up again before fixing on his mouth.

If Nick's black eyes hadn't been so hard, and his other features strongly masculine, his mouth might have made him into a pretty boy. Both his lips were full and sensual, curving around a mouthful of flashing white teeth, their perfection courtesy of the top-flight dentist her father had taken him to as soon as he'd been let out of prison.

If Sarah had any criticism, it was of his hair, which she believed he kept far too short. Still, the buzz-cut style did give him an intimidating look that probably worked well for him in the business world.

'Well, hello, stranger,' he said, his dark eyes sweeping down to her sneakered feet, then up again.

Not a hint of admiration in *his* expression, however, or even surprise. No reaction at all. Zilch.

His lack of reaction—she'd been expecting some sort of compliment—exasperated Sarah. What did she have to do to make the man notice her, damn it?

'Thanks, Jim,' he said, bending to pick up her bags. 'I'll take these now.'

'Yes, thanks, Jim,' Sarah managed to echo through clenched teeth.

Jim nodded, then moved off, by which time Nick had picked up her luggage and turned to carry it inside.

Sarah wanted to hit him. Instead, she gritted her teeth even harder.

Suddenly, she couldn't wait to turn twenty-five. The sooner she got Nick out of her life, the better. He was like a thorn in her side, niggling away at her. How could she have what she wanted most in life—which was children of her own—if he was always there, spoiling things for her? How could she feel completely happy when she kept comparing every man she dated to him?

Out of sight would be out of mind. Hopefully.

Sarah closed the front door after her,

smothering a sigh when she saw Nick heading for the stairs with her cases.

'I can take those up,' she said, desperately needing a few minutes away from the man to regain her composure.

As much as Sarah had subconsciously always known that nothing would ever come of her secret feelings for Nick, finally facing the futility of her fantasies was a soul-shattering experience.

He hadn't even noticed that she'd lost weight!

All that work. For *nothing*!

'It's no trouble,' he threw over his shoulder as he continued on up the stairs with the bags.

Sarah gritted her teeth, and hurried up the stairs after him. 'Why aren't you at golf?'

'I wanted the opportunity to talk to you,' he tossed back at her. 'Privately.'

'About what?'

He didn't answer her, instead charging on ahead with her bags.

'About what, Nick?' she repeated when she caught up, frustrated by his lack of reply.

He ground to a halt on the top landing, dropped her bags then turned to face her.

'Flora, for one thing.'

'What about her? She's not ill, is she?'

'No, but she can't do what she used to do. She gets very tired. This last year, I've had to hire a home-cleaning service to come in twice a week to do all the heavy cleaning for her.'

'I didn't realise.'

'If you came home occasionally,' Nick pointed out drily, 'you might have noticed.'

It was a fair comment, evoking a large dose of guilt. Sarah recognised she'd been very self-obsessed this past year. But she'd been on a mission. A futile mission, as it turned out.

'I…I've been very busy,' she said by way of an excuse.

'With the new boyfriend, I take it?' came his next comment, this one quite sarcastic.

Sarah bristled. 'I have a right to a social life,' she retorted, taking off her sunglasses so that she could glare at him. '*You* have one.'

'Indeed. But it doesn't take over my whole existence.'

His critical tone was so typical of Nick when it came to her having a boyfriend, his condemning attitude often sparking a reckless rebellion in her that had her running off at the mouth.

Today was no exception.

'Derek and I are very much in love. Something *you* could never identify with. When people are truly in love they want to spend every minute of every day with them.'

'I'm surprised you came home today at all, then,' he countered quite sharply. 'Or will your lover be dropping by later?'

Sarah flushed. 'Derek's working today.'

'Doing what?'

'He owns a gym.'

'Aah. That explains it.'

'Explains what?'

'Your new shape.'

So he *had* noticed! 'You say that like there's something wrong with it.'

'You looked fine the way you were.'

Sarah's mouth dropped open. 'You have to be joking! I was getting fat!'

'Don't be ridiculous.'

Sarah rolled her eyes. Either the man was blind, or he cared about her so little that he'd never really looked at her before.

'Maybe you just didn't notice.'

Nick gave an offhand shrug. 'Maybe I didn't. Still, I suppose it's not up to me to tell you what to do.'

'I'm glad you've finally realised that!'

'Meaning?'

'I couldn't count the number of times you've interfered in my life, and my relationships. Every time I brought a boyfriend home in the past, you went out of your way to make him feel stupid. And me to boot.'

'I was only doing what your father asked me to do, Sarah. Which was to protect you from the money-grubbing creeps in this world.'

'They weren't money-grubbing creeps!'

'Indeed they were.'

'I'll be the judge of that from now on, thank you very much.'

'Not till your twenty-fifth birthday, madam. I have no intention of letting you fall into the hands of some gold-digging gigolo at this late stage. I wouldn't be able to sleep at night if I did that.'

'Huh. I can't see you ever losing any sleep over me.'

'Then you'd be dead wrong, sweetheart,' he grated out.

Their eyes met, with Sarah sucking in sharply at the momentary fury she glimpsed in Nick's face. It came home to her then just how much he'd hated being her guardian all these years. No doubt he would be very relieved when she turned twenty-five next year and his obligation to her father was over.

'I haven't given you that much trouble, have I?' she said, her softer voice reflecting her drop in spirits.

As much as she accepted Nick would never be attracted to her, she'd always thought that, underneath everything, he liked her. Not just because she was her father's daughter, but because of the person she was. When she was younger, he'd often told her what a great kid she was. He'd said she had character, and a good heart. He'd also said she was fun to be with, proving it by spending a lot of his spare time with her.

Of course, that had been a long time ago, before Nick had become a success in his own right. When that started to happen, he'd begun to ignore her. Then, after her father died, the rot had set in completely. It was patently obvious that she was now reduced to nothing more than a responsibility, a responsibility that he obviously found both tedious and exasperating.

'Does he know how rich you're shortly going to be?' he demanded to know.

Sarah's mouth thinned. Here we go again, she thought angrily.

Yet there was no point in lying. Better she answer Nick's questions now than to have him put Derek through the third degree on Christmas Day.

'He knows I'm going to be rich,' she bit out. 'But he doesn't know the full extent of my inheritance.'

'He'll know once he shows up tomorrow. People who live in this street have to be multimillionaires at least. It won't take him long to put two and two together.'

'Derek's not a fortune-hunter, Nick. He's a very decent man.'

'How do you know?'

'I just know.'

'My God, you know nothing!' he flung at

her. 'Your father thought he was protecting you with his will. Instead, he set you up for disaster. He should have given most of his money away, donated it to some charity, not left it in the hands of a girl such as you.'

'What do you mean, a girl such as me?'

He opened his mouth to say something but then obviously thought better of it. Instead, he picked up her bags and carried them along the hallway to her room, the stiff set of his shoulders very telling. After dumping her cases just inside the door, he retreated back out into the hallway.

'We'll continue this discussion later,' he said in that deceptively quiet manner he always adopted on the odd occasion when he was in danger of losing his cool.

Over the years Sarah had learned to recognise this tactic of his. Nick hated losing his temper. Hated losing control. He preferred to act like the consummate ice-man, both professionally and personally. She'd rarely heard him yell. He didn't even swear any more, as he once had.

But his body language could speak volumes. So could his eyes.

Though not always. He did have the ability to make them totally unreadable. But not straight away. If you were watching him closely, you could sometimes glimpse what was going on in his head before he drew the blinds down.

'We'll have morning tea in the kitchen,' he pronounced, 'then we'll adjourn to my study and talk.'

'Not about Derek,' Sarah retorted. 'I have no intention of listening to you criticising someone you haven't even met.'

'Fair enough. But I have lots of other things to talk to you about, Sarah. Important issues connected with your inheritance. I want to have everything settled before Christmas.'

'But I don't turn twenty-five till February,' she protested. 'We have the rest of my summer break to settle things!'

'No, we don't. I won't be here.'

'Where will you be?'

'I'm spending most of January on Happy Island.'

Sarah's heart sank. She knew Nick had a holiday house there. But he rarely used it at this time of year.

'Flora never said anything about that when I called.'

'The subject probably didn't come up.'

'There's still the week between Christmas and New Year,' she argued, feeling very put out with Nick's choosing to go away for so long.

'Yes. But I'm having a guest stay during that week. And you have your new boy-friend, who you freely admit you wish to spend every minute of every day with. Better we settle everything whilst we have the chance.'

'But I have to decorate the tree today.'

'I just want a couple of hours, Sarah. Not all day.'

'What about tonight? Can't this wait till tonight?'

'I'm going present-shopping tonight.'

Sarah sighed. Wasn't that just like a man to go present-shopping at the last minute?

'Come on,' he said abruptly. 'Let's go downstairs.'

'I need to go to the bathroom first,' she said quite truthfully.

'Fine,' he replied with another offhand

shrug. 'I'll go ahead and tell Flora to put on the kettle.'

Sarah shook her head as she watched Nick go. Derek didn't know what he was talking about. Dolling herself up tomorrow and sucking up to a pretend boyfriend wasn't going to make a blind bit of difference. She was nothing to Nick but an obligation that he obviously wanted over and done with. It was clear to Sarah that he couldn't wait for her twenty-fifth birthday to arrive.

Suddenly, she felt the same way. She was sick and tired of letting her feelings for Nick distress her. Sick and tired of secretly pining for what would never be.

Time to move on, girl. Time to get yourself a life. One that doesn't include Nick!

CHAPTER THREE

FLORA was in the kitchen, cutting up the caramel slice she'd made that morning, when Nick walked in with a face like thunder.

'Wasn't that Sarah at the door?' she asked.

'Yep. She won't be long. You can put on the kettle.'

Flora turned to pop the caramel slice back in the fridge before switching on the electric kettle. 'It's good to have her home,' she said. 'Isn't it?'

Nick scowled as he slid onto one of the four stools fronting the black marble breakfast bar. 'Speak for yourself, Flora.'

'Come, now, Nick. You've missed her. You know you have.'

'I know no such thing. Ray was out of his mind to make me that girl's guardian. I'll breathe a huge sigh of relief when February comes round, I can tell you.'

'I suppose it has been a big responsibility,' Flora agreed. 'Especially considering how much money she's going to inherit. What do you make of this new boyfriend of hers? Do you think he's on the up and up?'

'Who knows?'

'It's strange that she hadn't mentioned him before last night, don't you think? It makes me wonder what's wrong with him.'

'I've just been thinking the same thing. I guess we'll just have to wait and see.'

'I guess so,' Flora said. 'So how does she look?'

'What do you mean?'

'She told me last night that she'd been exercising and had lost weight. Don't tell me you didn't notice.'

'Yeah, I noticed.'

'And?' Flora asked, exasperated with Nick's reluctance to elaborate. He was just as bad as Jim sometimes. Why was it that men didn't like to talk? It would be nice to have Sarah home, just so she had someone to chat with occasionally.

'I thought she looked fine the way she was.'

'Isn't that just like a man? They never want the women in their life to change. Aah, there she is, the girl herself. Come over here, love, and give old Flora a hug.'

Sarah's heart squeezed tight when Flora enveloped her into a tight embrace. It had been a long time since anyone had hugged her like that.

There'd been no hug from Nick this morning. Not even a peck on the cheek. He never touched her, except accidentally.

Her gaze slid over Flora's shoulder to land on the man himself. But he wasn't looking her way. He was staring down at the black bench top, looking highly disgruntled.

Probably wishing he were at golf.

'Oh, my,' Flora said when she finally held Sarah out at arm's length. 'You *have* lost quite a few pounds, haven't you? Still, now you can have a big piece of your favourite caramel slice without feeling guilty,' she added before turning away to open the fridge. 'I made it for you first thing this morning.'

'You shouldn't have, Flora,' Sarah chided, but gently.

'Nonsense. What else do I have to do? Did you know that the whole of the Christmas lunch is being catered this year? Nick says it's too much for me. All I'm allowed to do is make a couple of miserable puddings. I ask you!'

She rolled her eyes at Sarah, who was thinking to herself that Flora had aged quite a bit this past year. Her face was very lined and her hair had turned totally grey.

'Not that I'm complaining, Nick,' Flora went on. 'I do know I'm getting older. But I'm not totally useless yet. I could easily have baked a leg of pork and a turkey. And some nice hot veggies for those who don't like salad and seafood. Still, enough of that. What's done is done. Now, sit up there next to Nick, Sarah, and tell us all about your new boyfriend whilst I pour the tea.'

Sarah smothered a groan, but did as she was told, though she didn't sit right next to Nick, leaving one stool between them.

'What would you like to know?' she asked with brilliant nonchalance.

'How old is he, for starters?'

Sarah realised she had no idea.

'Thirty-five,' she guessed. One year younger than Nick.

Nick's head swung her way. 'Handsome?'

'Very. Looks like a movie star.'

Was she crazy, or did Nick's eyes glitter when she said that?

'How long have you been seeing each other?' Flora asked.

Sarah decided to use the truth as much as possible. 'We met shortly after last Easter. I hired him as my personal trainer.'

Nick made a small scoffing sound.

Sarah ignored him.

'Why haven't you mentioned him before?' Flora asked.

Sarah winced. She should have realised she'd get the third degree about Derek, from both Nick and Flora. Again, she decided to stick to the truth as closely as she could.

'We haven't been boyfriend and girlfriend all that time,' she replied. 'That's a more recent development. He asked me out for a drink one night after my workout, one thing led to another and…well, what can I say? I'm very happy.'

Sarah smiled, despite the lurch within her chest.

'And very healthy, too,' Flora said with a return smile. 'Don't you think so, Nick?'

'I think she looks like she could do with some of your caramel slice.'

Sarah found a laugh from somewhere. 'That's funny coming from you. All your girlfriends have figures like rakes.'

'Not *all* of them. You haven't met Chloe, have you?'

'I haven't had the pleasure yet.'

'You will. Tomorrow.'

'How nice.'

'You'll like her.'

'Oh, I doubt it. I never like any of your girlfriends, Nick. The same way you never like any of my boyfriends. I've already warned Derek.'

'Should I warn Chloe?'

Sarah shrugged. 'Why bother? It won't change anything.'

'Will you two stop bickering?' Flora

intervened. 'It's Christmas, the season of peace and love.'

Sarah almost pointed out that Nick didn't believe in love, but she held her tongue. Sniping at Nick was not in keeping with her resolution to move on. But he'd really got under her skin with his remarks about her being skinny.

When Flora presented a plate full of caramel slice right in front of her, she couldn't really refuse. But she did take the smallest piece and proceeded to eat it very slowly between long sips of tea. Nick chose the biggest portion, devoured it within seconds, then had the gall to take a second salivating slice. The lucky devil had one of those metabolisms that allowed him to eat whatever he liked without getting fat. Of course, he did work out with weights every other day, and swam a lot.

Although thirty-six now, he didn't carry an extra ounce of fat on his long, lean body. Really, other than some muscling up around his chest and arms, Nick hadn't changed much since the day they'd met.

Physically, that was. He'd changed a good

deal in other ways, matching his personality to suit whatever company he was in, sometimes warm and charming, at other times adopting a confident air of cool sophistication and *savoir-faire*, both personas a long way from the introverted and rather angry young man he'd been when he'd first come to live at Goldmine.

Though he was never angry with me, Sarah recalled. Never. He had always been sweet, kind and generous with his time. He'd made a lonely little girl's life much less lonely.

Oh, how she'd loved him for that!

Sarah much preferred the Nick of old to the one sitting beside her today.

In the beginning, when he'd launched himself into the business world, she'd admired his ambition. But success had made Nick greedy for the good life, feeding on hedonistic pleasures that were as fleeting as they were shallow. Other than the holiday house on Happy Island, he owned a penthouse on the Gold Coast and a chalet in the southern snowfields. When he wasn't working at making more money, he flitted from one to the other, always accompanied by his latest lady-love.

Whoops, no. Amend that to latest playmate. Love was never part of Nick's lifestyle.

Her father had always said how proud of Nick he was. He'd lauded Nick's work ethics, his intellect and his entrepreneurial vision.

Sarah could see that, professionally, there was much to be proud of. But surely her father would have been disappointed, if he'd been alive today, at the way Nick conducted his personal life. There was something reprehensible about a man whose girlfriends never lasted longer than six months, and who boasted that he would never marry.

No, that was unfair. Nick had never boasted about his inability to fall in love. He'd merely stated it as a fact.

Sarah had to concede that at least Nick was honest in his relationships. She felt positive he never spun any of his girlfriends a line of bull. They'd always known that their role in his life was strictly sexual and definitely temporary.

'Glad to see you're still capable of enjoying your food.'

Nick's droll remark jolted Sarah out of her reverie, her stomach contracting in horror once she realised she'd consumed a second piece of caramel slice without being aware of it.

She kept her cool, however, determined not to let Nick needle her further.

'Who could resist Flora's caramel slice?' she tossed at him airily. 'Next Christmas we'll get back to having a smaller Christmas lunch, Flora, and you can cook whatever you like.'

'You won't keep your father's tradition going?' Nick asked in a challenging voice.

'Is that what you think you've been doing, Nick?' she countered. 'When Dad was alive, Christmas lunch was a gathering of true friends, not a collection of business acquaintances.'

'Is that so? I think perhaps you're mistaken about that. Most of your father's so-called friends were business contacts.'

Nick was right, of course. But people had still liked her father for himself, not just for what they could get out of him. At least, she liked to think so.

But maybe she was wrong. Maybe she'd seen him through rose-coloured glasses. Maybe, underneath his *bonhomie*, he'd been as hard and cynical as Nick.

No, that wasn't true. He'd been a kind and generous man.

Not a brilliant dad, though. During her years at boarding-school he'd often made excuses for not being able to come to school functions, all of those excuses related to work. Then, when she came home for school holidays, she'd largely been left to her own devices.

If she was strictly honest, things hadn't been much better when her mother was still alive. A dedicated career woman, Jess Steinway had been totally unprepared for the sacrifices motherhood entailed upon the arrival of an unexpected baby at forty. Sarah had been raised by a succession of impersonal nannies till she went to kindergarten, after which Flora had taken over as carer before and after school. But Flora, warm and chatty though she was, had mostly been too busy with the house to do much more than feed Sarah and make sure she did her homework.

No one had spent quality time with her, or played with her, till Nick had come along.

She turned her head to look at him, a wave of sadness washing through her. Oh, how she wished he was still their chauffeur, and she the little girl who could love him without reservation.

Tears pricked at her eyes, right at that moment when Nick's head turned her way. She quickly blinked them away, but not before she glimpsed regret in his.

'Sorry,' he muttered. 'I didn't mean any disrespect for your father. He was a good man and a very generous one. Christmas was his favourite time of year. Did you know that every Christmas he gave huge donations to the various charities round Sydney for the homeless? Because of him, they always had a proper Christmas dinner. And no one, especially the children, went without a present.'

Sarah frowned. 'I didn't know that.' She knew about his good work with young pris-

'Why do you think I bought it?' Nick quipped. 'Had to do something to stop my right-hand man from spending every summer's day glued to that TV, when he should be outside working. My motivation was purely selfish, I assure you. And don't be expecting anything too expensive for Christmas, because I'm flat broke now.'

'Oh, go on with you,' Flora said laughingly.

'Don't laugh. I've made two dud movies already this year. And I'm damned worried about the one coming out in the New Year. We've had a couple of test audiences view it and they said the ending was way too sad. The director reluctantly agreed to reshoot it with a happy ending, but I've decided to go with his original vision. If this one flops, I might have to come to Sarah here for a loan.'

Sarah was shocked by this news. She knew better than anyone that Nick's ego would not survive becoming poor again. 'I can give you as much as you need, come February. And it won't be a loan, either.'

'Lord, what am I going to do with this girl, Flora? I hope you haven't made any similar offers to this boyfriend of yours.

Don't ever give a man money, Sarah,' he told her sternly. 'It brings out the worst in them.'

Sarah shook her head at him. 'How many times do I have to tell you? Derek doesn't want my money.'

'He will, when he sees how much you've got.'

'Not every man is a fortune-hunter, Nick. Now, if you don't mind, I do not wish to discuss Derek any further. I know there's no convincing you that no man could possibly love me for myself and not my money, so I'd prefer not to try.'

'Hear hear,' Flora agreed. 'I agree with Sarah. Another piece of caramel slice, love?'

The ringing of Nick's cellphone was a welcome interruption, not only to his incessant questioning about Derek, but also to her escalating exasperation. Tomorrow was not going to be a pride-saving exercise. It was going to be hell!

'Hi there,' she heard Nick say in that voice he reserved for girlfriends. 'Yeah, that'd be great, Chloe. OK. I'll pick you up tonight at seven. Bye.'

He clicked off his phone and slipped off the stool. 'Sorry, folks. Change of plan. Chloe's had a last-minute invitation to a Christmas Eve party at some bigwig's place, so I'll have to dash out and do my present-shopping now. We'll have to put off that talk till I get back, Sarah.'

'Fine,' she said, pretending not to care. But she did. She cared a lot. Not about the talk so much but about his going out this afternoon, then going out with Chloe tonight. Pathetic, really. The way she would accept the crumbs of his company.

'Don't forget I want a new car,' Sarah called after him as he walked away. 'A yellow one.'

Nick stopped walking, then glanced over his shoulder at her. 'Yellow,' he repeated drily. 'Any particular make?'

She named a top-of-the-range model. 'Of course. What else?'

When he smiled his amusement at her, Sarah's heart lightened a little. It was still there, that special bond between them. Because they *knew* each other.

Chloe didn't know Nick. Not the real him.

She only knew the man who had graced the cover of Australia's leading financial newspaper last year.

'I'll see what I can do,' he said. 'Bye, girls.'

'Bye,' Sarah trilled back, smiling on the outside whilst inside she was already sinking back into the pit, that moment of pleasurable intimacy wiped away in the face of where Nick would be going tonight.

Do not succumb to jealousy, she lectured herself, or depression. Do not let him do this to you!

'You don't still have a thing for Nick, do you, love?'

Flora's softly delivered question was almost Sarah's undoing.

Gulping down the sudden lump in her throat, she straightened her spine and adopted what she hoped was a believable expression. 'No, of course not.'

'That's good. Because it would be a mistake. There's no future for any woman with a man like Nick.'

Sarah laughed a dry little laugh. 'Don't you think I know that, Flora?'

'This Derek chap, is it serious between you two?'

Sarah hesitated to answer for a second too long.

'I didn't think so,' Flora said. 'You would have told me about him sooner, if that were the case.'

'Don't tell Nick,' she blurted out.

Flora's eyes narrowed. 'Is this Derek a real boyfriend or not?'

Sarah bit her bottom lip. She knew it would be wiser to lie, but she couldn't, not to Flora's face.

'He…he's just a friend.'

Flora gave her a long, searching look. 'What game are you playing at, girlie?'

Sarah sighed. 'Nothing bad, Flora. I just wanted to bring someone to the Christmas lunch and Derek volunteered. I'm sick and tired of Nick's girlfriends looking down their noses at me.'

'So it's a matter of female pride, is it?'

'Yes; yes, that's exactly what it is.'

'You do realise Nick is going to give this poor Derek the third degree?'

'Yes, he's prepared for that.'

Flora pulled a face. 'I hope so. Because Nick takes his job as your guardian very seriously, love.'

'Derek can hold his own.'

'None of your other boyfriends could.'

'Derek's not a real boyfriend.'

'But he's pretending to be one.'

'Yes.'

Flora sighed. 'Good luck to him, then. That's all I can say.'

CHAPTER FOUR

SARAH decorated the Christmas tree on automatic pilot, her mind still on Flora's last words.

Flora was right, of course. Derek was going to be in for a rough time tomorrow.

But I did warn him, she reminded herself. And he still wanted to do it. In fact, he seemed to find the prospect of pretending to be my boyfriend an exciting challenge.

Sarah was beginning to find the thought terrifying. Nightmarish possibilities kept popping into her mind. What if Nick somehow discovered that Derek was gay? Or that their so-called relationship was just a sham? How could she explain such a crazy deception? Surely saving her pride wasn't worth the risk of feeling more of a fool in front of him.

And in front of Chloe.

Chloe…

Already she didn't like the woman and she hadn't even met her.

Nick had implied earlier that Chloe wasn't as skinny as his usual girlfriend. Was she blonde as well?

She would have to ask Flora later for a more detailed description.

Finally, all of the ornaments and lights were hung, except for the star that went on top of the tree. A glance at her watch showed that it was ten past six, way past time for a toasted sandwich and some coffee. She'd bypassed lunch after having eaten two pieces of that dreaded caramel slice, believing that they would easily sustain her for the whole afternoon.

Serious hunger pangs told her she'd been wrong. But the Christmas star came first.

Sarah climbed up the stepladder once more, this time having to go up on tiptoe to reach the right spot.

'That's a great-looking tree.'

Sarah jumped at the unexpected sound of Nick's voice, the star dropping from her hands as the back feet of the ladder lifted off the floor and she began to overbalance forwards. How Nick managed to save her she'd never know, but one second she was about to crash head-first into the tree, the next the ladder was abruptly righted and she fell backwards into Nick's arms.

'Oh, lord!' she gasped, her arms flailing wide whilst his wound tightly around her back, pulling her hard against his chest.

'You're all right,' he told her.

Her arms finally found a home around his neck, her heart thudding loudly behind her ribs.

'You…you frightened the life out of me,' she blurted out.

'Sorry. Didn't mean to.'

Sarah opened her mouth to say something more, *anything* to defuse the excitement that had instantly been sparked by finding herself in Nick's embrace. Such physical closeness, however, was not conducive to sensible brain activity, her mind going totally blank when his dark eyes dropped down to her softly parted lips.

For several, highly charged seconds Nick just stared at them.

Time seemed to slow around her, the air stilling whilst her pounding heart suspended its beat, her eyes closing as her head tipped invitingly sideways.

He was going to kiss her. She was sure of it!

To suddenly find herself being lowered onto her feet came as a shock.

'Oh,' she cried out, her eyes flying open to discover Nick frowning down at her with nothing but concern in his face.

'Steady now,' he said.

Sarah could have cried. Clearly, she was so *desperate* in her infatuation with this man that she'd conjured up passion where there was none. Not on his part, anyway.

'I'm fine, thank you,' she said curtly, pride demanding she cool her overheated blood and still that foolish, treacherous heart of hers.

'For a second there, I thought you were going to faint.'

'Faint? Why on earth would I faint?'

'Some girls do, after a shock.'

'I'm fine,' she reiterated.

'In that case, how about thanking me for saving you from a nasty fall?'

'Which you caused in the first place,' she pointed out stroppily. 'What are you doing home, anyway? I thought you were going to a party at seven. It's not far off that now.'

'Chloe forgot to tell me that it was black-tie. So I came home to change.'

Sarah had seen Nick in a dinner suit. Of course, he looked devastatingly handsome. Jealousy jabbed at her as she thought of Chloe on his arm tonight, then possibly in his bed…

Sarah's stomach somersaulted at the thought.

'I'm surprised you're not going out tonight yourself,' Nick said.

'What? Oh, yes, well…Derek wanted to take me somewhere, but I…I told him I'd be too busy with the tree and present-wrapping.' She was babbling and stammering! Why, oh, why did she have to think about Nick with Chloe?

'You should do what I do,' Nick said. 'Only buy presents at shops that do free gift-wrapping.'

And in shops where some smitten female sales assistant did all the choosing for him as well, Sarah thought ruefully.

'I'd better get going,' Nick went on. 'See you at present-opening in the morning. And before you ask, no, Chloe will not be in attendance. So you won't have to sulk.'

'I never sulk,' Sarah snapped.

'Oh, yes, you do, madam. But I agree with you on one score: some of my girlfriends have not been all that nice to you. Still, that's because most of them are jealous.'

'Of *me*?' Sarah could not have been more surprised.

Nick's smile was wry. 'How would you like to discover that your Derek was living with an attractive young female ward? Now I really must go,' he pronounced abruptly, and spun away.

'We still haven't had that private talk,' she called after him.

He stopped and glanced over his shoulder at her, his body language impatient. 'I realise that. It'll just have to wait till after Christmas Day.'

'But won't Chloe be here then?'

Nick had said this morning that he had a guest between Christmas and New Year. Who other than his current girlfriend?

'Chloe and I don't need to spend every minute of every day together,' he said rather pointedly. 'See you in the morning, Sarah.'

Sarah watched him stride across the family room, then leap up the two steps that led to the foyer. She heard him run up the stairs, depression descending at the sound of his hurrying to take out his girlfriend.

'I'm glad Derek is coming tomorrow,' she muttered under her breath.

'Talking to yourself is never a good idea, love.'

Sarah turned, then smiled at Flora. 'I have some of my best conversations with myself.'

'Better than that tea towel you used to talk to when you were a child, I suppose.'

Sarah stared at Flora. 'You knew about that?'

'Nothing much gets by me, love. So was the tea towel your other self? Or a special friend?'

'A special friend,' she confessed.

'Boy or girl?'

'Um…boy. Sort of.'

'He wasn't called Nick, was he?'

Sarah flushed.

'Like I said, love,' Flora continued as she went over and turned the switch that lit up the tree, 'nothing much gets by me. My, now, that is one lovely tree.'

'Jim chose a really good one this year.'

'He did indeed. Was that Nick I heard a minute ago?'

'Yes. He came home to change. The party's black-tie.'

'I'm not surprised. Chloe's a social climber, if ever there was one.'

Sarah shook her head. 'She sounds awful. What on earth does Nick see in her?'

'What does Nick see in any of his girlfriends? I suppose he doesn't much care about their characters as long as they're beautiful and do whatever he wants them to do in bed. He doesn't keep any of them, after all.'

'Flora! I've never heard you talk like this about Nick before.'

Flora shrugged. 'I'm getting old, I guess. When you get old you say things you wouldn't dare say before. Don't get me wrong. I'm very fond of Nick. But where women are concerned, he's bad news. He's never made a pass at you, has he, Sarah?'

'What? Me? No, never!'

'Just as well, with you having that crush on him.'

'I'm over that now.'

'You might think you are, but he'd still be able to turn your head, if he tried.'

Flora had never said a truer word. 'Why would he bother, when he has the likes of Chloe in his bed?'

Flora wrinkled her nose. 'I suspect Madame Chloe is fast reaching her use-by date. I'd watch myself, if I were you, when you swan downstairs tomorrow wearing one of those sexy new dresses of yours.'

Sarah's mouth dropped open. 'How do you know about them?'

'Couldn't sit around doing nothing all afternoon, so I unpacked for you. Which one are you wearing tomorrow? The red and white one, I'll bet.'

'Flora, you're an old sticky-beak!'

Flora remained quite nonplussed at this

accusation. 'How do you think I get to know everything? I also put all those lovely Christmas cards you got from your pupils on your dressing table. Didn't leave room for much else, I'm afraid, so I set out all your new make-up and perfume and skin-care stuff on the vanity unit in your bathroom.'

Sarah didn't know whether to be appreciative, or annoyed. 'So, did everything get your seal of approval?'

'Let's just say I think you'll give Chloe a run for her money in the beauty stakes.'

'I sure hope so.'

'And who knows? Maybe your Derek will take one look at you and decide to take your friendship to a different level.

'Somehow I don't think that's likely to happen.'

'You never know, love. You just never know.'

CHAPTER FIVE

SARAH woke to a less than gentle shake of her shoulder and an unshaven Nick leaning over her. Surprise and shock sent her eyes instantly wide and her heart racing.

'What is it?' she exclaimed. 'What's wrong?'

When he straightened she saw he was already dressed, in jeans and a T-shirt. 'Nothing's *wrong*,' he said.

Then what on earth was he doing in her bedroom at some ungodly hour in the morning?

'Flora sent me to wake you,' he went on, his voice carrying a measure of exasperation.

'What for?' Confusion in her own voice.

'For breakfast and present-giving.'

Sarah blinked. '*This* early?'

'The men with the tables and blinds are due to arrive at nine and it's already eight.'

'Eight!' Sarah sat bolt upright, pushing her hair back from her face as she glanced first at her sun-drenched balcony, then at her bedside clock, which confirmed that it was indeed, just after eight. Yet she had set her alarm for six, wanting to be looking her very best for present-opening with her hair done, make-up perfect and dressed to impress in her sexy new jeans and a very pretty green top.

'I must have slept through the alarm,' she said with a groan.

Or perhaps she'd fallen asleep without actually setting it. She'd stayed up quite late, doing everything she could the night before in preparation for Christmas Day.

'Just get up and come downstairs,' Nick said impatiently before whirling and striding from the room.

'I…I'll be down shortly,' she called after him.

'You'd better be,' he called back.

It wasn't till Nick left that Sarah realised she hadn't wished him a happy Christmas. Still, he hadn't thought to wish her the season's greetings, either. He'd sounded tired and grumpy. Probably hadn't had enough sleep. She hadn't heard him come in last night, so it had to have been very late. Probably went to Chloe's place after the party and…

'Don't think about last night,' she lectured herself aloud. 'Just get up and get on with things.'

Scooping in a deep breath, Sarah threw back the bedclothes and dashed into the bathroom, where she washed and cleaned her teeth in two minutes flat.

Then she stared at herself in the mirror.

D-Day, she thought with a wild fluttering in the stomach.

In a way it was a good thing that she didn't have time to dress. It would make her transformation later on all the more eye-catching and dramatic.

At the same time, she didn't want to look a total dag.

No time to do much with her hair except brush it, then twist it up into a loose knot on top of her head. Definitely no time for make-up.

Thankfully, her nightie was new and pretty, a lavender satin petticoat that had a matching robe. She slipped the robe on, looped the sash belt and hurried back into her bedroom, only then realising she had nothing suitable for her feet.

She never wore slippers. Sandals didn't seem right and neither did her flip-flops.

Oh, well, it wouldn't be the first time she went downstairs for Christmas breakfast barefooted and in her night things, though usually the latter were a bit longer. This nightie only reached mid-thigh, the robe to her knees. She would have to watch herself when she sat down. At least her legs were nice and smooth, all the way up. Sarah had taken herself off to a beautician late last week and had a full wax. Painful, but worth every penny not to have to worry about shaving for ages.

It felt a bit odd when she wasn't wearing panties, however. Like now, for instance.

Sarah might have slipped some panties on, but there really wasn't time for any more delay. It was already seven minutes past eight. And it wasn't as though anyone would know.

Sarah sucked in one last, long, calming breath, exhaled slowly, then set forth for the staircase.

Breakfast on Christmas morning was always very light; croissants and coffee served in front of the tree during present-opening. The family room in Goldmine was huge, with three distinct sitting areas. The Christmas tree was always placed down the far end, where there were two brown leather sofas facing each other, and a sturdy wooden coffee-table between them.

Everything was set out in readiness by the time Sarah made it downstairs, delicious aromas hitting her nostrils as she padded down the steps into the family room.

Her entry was quiet, due to her bare feet, giving her a second or two to survey the situation and work out in advance where she would sit.

Flora and Jim occupied opposite ends of the sofa facing the terrace, with Nick sitting in the middle of the sofa opposite, sipping coffee. She didn't want to sit next to him, not after what had happened yesterday. She certainly didn't want to sit next to him without her panties on. Physical proximity to Nick made her body—and her mind—go absolutely haywire.

Whilst Sarah was still resolved to go through with her plan to doll herself up for Christmas lunch—and to pretend Derek was her new boyfriend—she no longer held any hope whatsoever that Nick's eyes would be opened to her attractions as a female. She'd come to the dampening conclusion that after her father died Nick had mentally placed her in a box marked 'legal responsibility', thereby killing off any possibility of a personal relationship between them.

Suddenly his head turned her way, his dark eyes travelling swiftly from her tousled hair down to her scarlet toenails before moving back up again.

Was she mistaken, or did his eyes stop to linger on her breasts?

Whatever, her body responded instantly, a tingling feeling spreading over her skin whilst her heartbeat quickened and her nipples peaked alarmingly against the satin.

Sarah swallowed. Surely she was imagining it, as she'd imagined yesterday that he'd been going to kiss her. Yes, of course she was. The man was just looking, the way any man would when a pretty young female presented herself in front of him in her night things. He'd always *looked* at her, just not the way she wanted him to.

'Merry Christmas, everyone!' she trilled, determined not to let the deluding nature of her feelings for Nick spoil present-opening.

Flora and Jim glanced round at once, their kind faces breaking into warm smiles.

'And merry Christmas to you too, love,' Flora returned happily. 'Come on, come over here and sit next to me,' she said, patting the spot next to her.

'Sorry to keep you waiting.' Sarah angled herself past Flora's plump knees to take her place in the middle of the sofa directly opposite Nick. 'I must have slept through my alarm,' she added, once she was safely leaning back with her knees modestly pressed together and her robe arranged to cover as much of her bare thighs as possible.

'That's perfectly all right, love,' Flora said.

'You're here now. Coffee?' she offered, already leaning forward to pick up the coffee-pot.

'Yes, please.' Ignoring Nick—whose eyes had remained on her as she sat down—Sarah picked up a bread plate and helped herself to a croissant. 'Have you all eaten yet?'

'Jim and I have,' Flora said. 'Nick hasn't. He said he wasn't hungry. But I think he's got a hangover.'

'I do *not* have a hangover,' Nick protested. 'I feel fine. I'm just saving my appetite for lunch. But I will have a top-up of coffee, Flora,' he said, putting his mug on the coffee-table and pushing it towards her. 'With cream and sugar. That should keep me going for the next couple of hours.'

'Did you enjoy yourself at the party last night?' Sarah asked before she could snatch the words back. Truly, she was stupid some-times.

Nick picked up his refilled coffee mug and took an appreciative sip before answer-ing. 'It was a typical party of that type. To be honest, I think I'm partied out at the moment. That's one of the reasons I'm going to Happy Island. So that I can relax and do absolutely nothing for a while.'

'You could do absolutely nothing here,' Sarah pointed out, still hating the thought of his going away.

His dark eyes connected with hers over the rim of the mug. 'I can't, actually.'

'Why not?'

'People will bother me here,' he stated matter-of-factly.

And get in the way of your spending private time with your girlfriend.

Sarah could picture them skinny-dipping in his swimming pool on Happy Island, making leisurely love in the water and everywhere else in the no doubt luxurious holiday house.

It was a depressing train of thought.

'I think we should get on with present-giving,' Flora suggested. 'Jim, why don't you play Santa this year? Is that OK with you, Sarah?'

'Sure.' She was more than happy to sit there and devour her croissant, telling herself all the while that she would stop at just one. Because if she didn't, she'd be on her way back to Blubbersville.

But she needed the comfort the croissant gave her, needed to combat the dismay which was crushing her at that moment.

It was all so hopeless, Sarah thought wretchedly as she finished the first croissant in no time flat, then picked up another. Nick was never going to be hers. Not in bed, or anywhere else.

But then, you knew that, didn't you? You were a fool to listen to Derek, even for a moment.

Flora's gentle hand on her arm stopped her from stuffing the second croissant into her mouth.

'Perhaps that can wait till after we've opened the presents,' she suggested. 'Pick one of Nick's presents first, Jim, so that Sarah can drink her coffee.'

'Thank you, Flora,' Sarah whispered under her breath as she put down the croissant and picked up her coffee instead.

Jim rose and began moving the pile of presents around, Sarah's stomach contracting when he selected a smallish rectangular gift, wrapped in sparkling gold paper that had Christmas trees all over it.

'That's from me,' she said with false brightness when Jim handed it over to Nick.

Instead of Sarah feeling joyful anticipation at Nick's opening her present, her main emotion now was anxiety over his reaction. Sarah knew he would like it. She just hoped he wouldn't read anything into it. She would hate him to guess how she secretly felt about him. Hate the humiliation that would go with any such discovery.

Nick put down his coffee and ripped off the wrapping paper, frowning when confronted with the plain white cardboard box.

'Not cologne this year?' he said as he struggled to open the tight top, his short nails not helping with the task.

'No,' she replied. 'Do you want me to open it for you?'

'No. I'll get it. Eventually. There. Done.' Nick frowned some more as he upended the box and slid the bubble-wrapped gift into the palm of his hand. 'I have no idea what this could be,' he said with genuine puzzlement in his voice as he unwrapped it.

Sarah found herself holding her breath, rewarded when she saw pure, unadulterated delight fill his face.

'I…I hope you like it,' Sarah said, her cheeks colouring when his eyes lifted to stare over at her. Oh, goodness, she hoped he wasn't jumping to any embarrassing conclusions.

'What is it?' Flora piped up before Nick could answer her. 'Show me.'

Nick placed the miniature golf bag on the coffee-table for everyone to see before shaking his head at her.

'Words fail me, Sarah,' he said. But with amazement, not speculation.

'Look at this, Jim,' Flora said. 'It's a tiny little golf bag, full of the most beautiful little golf clubs.'

Jim leant over to take a closer look. 'It looks expensive.'

'Yes,' Nick agreed. 'It does. You shouldn't have spent so much money on me, Sarah.'

'Oh, it wasn't too dear for a soon-to-be heiress,' she replied airily. 'I thought you deserved something special for having put up with me all these years. The clubs are made from real silver, you know. English silver. They have hallmarks on them.'

'Where on earth did you get it?' Nick asked.

'I bought it on eBay. They have things you just don't see in the shops.'

'It's an exquisite and thoughtful present,' he said as he picked it up again. 'I'll treasure it always.'

Sarah's heart swelled with pleasure. If nothing else, she'd pleased him with her gift today, his genuinely warm reaction lifting her spirits and making her realise that he did care about her. She'd seen the affection in his eyes just now.

If she could not spark his sexual interest, then she would settle for his affection. It was better than nothing. For a while there, over the last few years, she'd begun thinking he didn't even like her any more.

But it was clear that he did. Maybe, once she grew up and got over this mad sexual obsession that had been tormenting her for far too long, they could even become friends again.

'Now it's your turn,' Nick said. 'Jim, give me that box with the red bow on it, please. Yes, that's the one.'

Nick smiled as he handed Sarah the store-wrapped package. 'Sorry it's not quite what you asked for.'

'What are you talking out? Oh, you mean the car. Well, I was only joking, you know. I can't imagine what you've bought me,' she said a bit breathlessly as she removed the bow then lifted the lid off the box.

Inside was a yellow car. A model of the one she'd mentioned to Nick. Not a minia-ture, but quite a large one. And not cheap, either.

Sarah laughed as she drew it out. 'Look what the wicked devil bought.'

Flora clucked her tongue at Nick. Jim liked it, though, calling it a beauty.

'If you open the driver's door,' Nick said, 'you might find something of more use to a soon-to-be heiress.'

Sarah did as she was told, and discovered a small, rectangular-shaped box made in dark red velvet. She knew, before she opened it, that it contained jewellery, but what?

Nerves claimed her stomach when she started to lift the lid. Nick never bought her jewellery. So why had he this time?

The sight of what was inside took her breath away.

'Oh, my God!' she gasped before gazing with wide eyes up at Nick. 'Tell me they're not real diamonds. Tell me they're zircons, or cut glass.'

'Of course they're real diamonds,' Flora said, leaning over to gaze at Sarah's present.

'They do look expensive,' Jim said, not for the first time that morning.

'Don't you like them?' Nick said drily. 'If you want to return them, I'm sure I still have the receipt somewhere.'

'Over my dead body!' Sarah retorted, snapping the box shut and hugging it to her chest.

Nick smiled. 'I do realise that you have all your mother's jewellery, but what suits one woman doesn't necessarily suit another. I thought these were more you.'

Sarah opened the box again, then picked one of the earrings out of the box for closer viewing. It had a large diamond at the lobe, and two dangling drops of smaller diamonds that shimmered and sparkled with the slightest movement.

'You think I'm a girl who favours flashy jewellery?'

'Diamonds aren't flashy, they're classy. And they never go out of fashion. You can wear them with any outfit.'

'Then I'll wear them today,' she decided immediately. 'To the Christmas lunch.' And I'll make sure Chloe knows who gave them to me, she vowed with uncharacteristic bitchiness.

'Yes, do that,' he agreed, an odd glitter in his eyes.

Sarah wished she knew what was going on in his head. But he was a closed book when he wanted to be.

'I'd like my present from Nick now,' Flora piped up.

'Oooh, did I get diamonds, too?' she added when Jim handed her a beautifully wrapped gift that was almost as small as Sarah's.

'Sorry,' Nick returned. 'I thought you'd prefer sapphires, to go with your pretty blue eyes.'

'Oh, go on with you,' Flora said laughingly.

But he *had* bought her sapphires, in the form of an utterly stunning, sapphire-encrusted watch. Jim got a watch, too, a very expensive gold one. Both were thrilled to pieces.

Sarah had never known Nick spend so much money on Christmas presents. He couldn't possibly be having serious financial worries, she thought with some relief, if he was throwing money around like this.

Flora and Jim seemed to like the gifts Sarah had chosen for them, Flora gushing over her favourite perfume and a cookbook, a new one that featured healthy meals. Jim was notoriously difficult to buy presents for, but a bottle of really rare port, plus a special glass engraved with his name, found favour.

In return, Flora and Jim gave Sarah a truly beautiful photo frame and a lovely feminine diary for the following year. It had pictures of flowers on every page, along with a special thought for the day. Nick became the proud owner of a new leather wallet, along with a very stylish gold silk tie.

'For the rare occasions when you're forced to wear one,' Flora informed him.

Which was, indeed, rare. Nick looked drop-dead gorgeous in a tux, or any suit for that matter. But he hated wearing them. He much preferred casual clothes. When circumstance demanded, he did wear a business suit, but he mostly teamed it with an open-necked shirt, or a crew-necked designer top. Only when protocol insisted on a tie did he wear one.

Around the house, he lived in shorts and jeans. Like now. Of course, he would change for Christmas lunch into a smart pair of trousers and an open-necked shirt, its length of sleeve depending on the weather. Today the forecast was for twenty-eight degrees, a very pleasant temperature for this time of year.

Sarah was glad it wasn't going to be cool, or rainy, as she would have frozen in her outfit.

'OK, folks,' Nick said, and abruptly stood up. 'Time to clean up the mess we've made here and shake a leg. Jim, I'll need your help getting everything ready outside. But Flora, you're not to rush around working yourself into a lather like you usually do. The caterers are due here at ten. All they require is a clean kitchen. They're providing everything, right down to the crockery, cutlery and glasses. Though not the wine. I bought that last week and stored it in the cellar. Jim, we'll need to bring that up as well. I'll put my presents away first, then meet you on the back terrace in five minutes. The guests are due to arrive from midday on, so, Sarah, leave plenty of time to dress and be back downstairs by five to twelve, ready to help me greet people at the door as they arrive.'

'How many are coming this year?' she asked.

'Twenty, if they all show up. Twenty-four, including us. OK?'

'Fine.'

They all rose to do as they were told, Sarah's heart beating faster when she thought of what lay ahead. Ok, so maybe it had been foolhardy of her to go along with Derek's plan without thinking it fully through, but now that the moment was at hand, it was still better than facing Christmas lunch alone. If nothing else, Derek wouldn't let her eat everything in sight.

But would he be able to withstand Nick's scrutiny?

Flora had told her yesterday that Nick took his job as her guardian very seriously indeed. Which in the past had obviously included vetting her boyfriends and making sure they weren't fortune-hunters.

Bringing Derek home so close to her inheriting her father's estate—not to mention telling Nick that they were very much in love—would only make him extra-protective. And paranoid.

She'd feel more confident if Derek weren't gay. And if she'd met this Chloe before. The unknown made her nervous. And she didn't want to be nervous. She wanted to swan downstairs just before midday, the epitome of cool composure and worldly sophistication. She wanted Nick to take one look at her and think to himself that she was the most beautiful and desirable woman that he had ever seen!

CHAPTER SIX

BY ELEVEN, Nick had done everything that needed to be done downstairs. The tables and shady blinds had been set up, and the wine brought up from the cellar and delivered to the family-room bar. The caterers had arrived right on ten, the staff consisting of three females and two males, a highly efficient group of people whose job it was to take the stress out of Christmas Day dinners.

Nick smiled ruefully to himself as he went upstairs. He had no doubt that they did a very good job with the food, the serving and the clearing up afterwards. But nothing—and no one—was going to take the stress out of *this* Christmas dinner. Not for him, anyway.

He'd thought he'd finally got a handle on

the unwanted desires Sarah had been evoking in him since she turned sixteen. But no, he'd just been deluding himself. Her staying away from home for most of this year had lulled him into a false sense of security. That, and meeting Chloe, whose sexy body and entertaining company had banished his secret lust for Sarah into the dungeon of his mind; that dark, dank place in which Nick imprisoned memories and emotions that were best forgotten. Or, at least, ignored.

He'd honestly thought he was prepared for Sarah's presence at Christmas. Thought he'd taken every precaution to keep the door to that mental dungeon firmly locked.

It had been Flora's news over breakfast yesterday that Sarah was bringing a boyfriend to the Christmas Day lunch which had shattered his illusion of iron self-control, stirring up a hornet's nest of jealousy within him. Next thing Nick knew, he was staying home from golf, just so that he could be here when she arrived. He'd made the excuse that he needed to talk to her about her inheritance, when in fact what he'd wanted most was to question her about the new man in her life.

Finding out that she was madly in love with this Derek didn't do his jealousy any good. OK, so on the surface he'd managed to control himself around Sarah. He gave himself full marks for not kissing her when he'd had the chance yesterday afternoon.

But he'd given in to temptation over those diamond earrings, hadn't he? Spent a small fortune on them, with the full intention of letting dear Derek know who'd bought them for her.

The truth was Nick had behaved badly every time Sarah brought home a boyfriend. He'd always pretended to himself that he was only doing what Ray had asked him to do, justifying his actions with the excuse that he was protecting her from fortune-hunters.

But that was actually far from the truth. None of those poor boys in the past had been gold-diggers. How could they be, when Sarah had never told anyone she was an heiress? They'd just been young men who'd had the good fortune—or was it misfortune?—to be where Nick had always wanted to be.

With Sarah.

The savage satisfaction he'd experienced every time he broke up one of her relationships showed just what kind of man he was: rotten to the core and wickedly selfish.

What would he do this time? he wondered grimly as he mounted the top landing and gazed down the hallway towards Sarah's bedroom.

Nothing, he hoped. The same way he'd done nothing yesterday when she'd been in his arms. He'd wanted to kiss her. Hell, he'd *ached* to kiss her.

But what would that have achieved, except make her look at him not with adoration as she'd once done, but with disgust? Sarah had finally fallen in love; possibly she was on the verge of having what she'd always wanted: marriage and children.

If this Derek was a decent fellow, then it would be cruel and callous to try to put doubts in Sarah's head about him.

Yet he wanted to…

Still, wanting to do something and

actually doing it were two entirely different things. He'd wanted to seduce Sarah for years, but he hadn't, had he?

Nick shook his head agitatedly as he forged on across the carpeted landing into the master bedroom. It wasn't till he shut the door behind him that his mind shifted from his immediate problem with Sarah to another problem he would have to face in the near future.

Come February, he had to leave this house.

It would be a terrible wrench, Nick knew. He'd grown very attached to the place, and the people in it. He could not imagine coming home to any other house, or any other bedroom.

Strange, really. Eight years ago, after Ray died and Nick moved into the house, he hadn't much liked this bedroom.

Ray had gone Japanese-mad after his trip to Tokyo; the gardens hadn't been the only thing around Goldmine to be changed: the master-bedroom suite had been totally gutted, its walls painted white, the plush gold carpet ripped out and polished floorboards laid. The heavy mahogany bedroom suite had been given to charity, to be replaced by black lacquered Japanese-style furniture. The king-sized bed was now large and low, the duvet and pillows covered in scarlet silk with sprays of flowers at their corners.

Other than two matching black lacquered bedside tables, there'd been no furniture in the room, the walk-in wardrobe being spacious enough to accommodate all Ray's clothes.

The bathroom had been changed with an all-white suite during this refurbishment, enlarged as well to accommodate a huge spa bath that you could practically swim in.

Nick liked the bathroom, but had found the bedroom rather stark, and not evocative of the atmosphere he wanted his bachelor boudoir to evoke. So he'd bought three fluffy white rugs to surround the bed, and some white cane chairs for the corners. A huge plasma television now hung on the wall opposite the bed with access to every satellite television channel available. Black silk sheets were his final purchases, along with some new shades for the chrome-based bedside lamps: red, of course.

The effect at night was erotic and sensual.

When in his bedroom, Nick didn't pretend to be anything but what he was: a very sensual man.

Which made his actions last night after the party almost incomprehensible.

Why, when he'd taken Chloe home, hadn't he gone inside and made mad, passionate love to her? She'd been all over him like a rash at the door. Normally, he loved it when she was sexually aggressive, loved it that he didn't have to be gentle with her. At any other time, he would have pushed her inside and had her up against the wall.

Instead her rapacious mouth had repelled him for some reason, and he found himself telling her he had a headache. A *headache*, for pity's sake!

Chloe had been surprised, but reasonably understanding, sending him off with a kiss on the cheek and the advice to have a good night's sleep.

'You won't get off so easily tomorrow night,' she'd added as he walked back to his car.

Nick hadn't gone straight home. He'd

driven round and round, trying to work out why he wasn't in Chloe's bed right at that moment, sating his desires to a degree where he wouldn't be capable of feeling any lust for anyone!

Then, when he'd finally come home, he'd fallen into a fitful sleep, his dreams filled with disturbingly erotic images involving the bane of his life. In one dream, Sarah had come down to the Christmas lunch wearing that minute bikini that had tormented him all those years ago. In another, she had been decorating that damned Christmas tree in the nude. In yet another, she'd been in his arms and he was kissing her the way he'd wanted to kiss her yesterday.

He'd woken from that dream incredibly aroused.

When Flora had sent him into Sarah's bedroom to wake her this morning, he'd stared down at her sleeping form for longer than was decent, the dungeon door in his mind well and truly open. Then, when she'd waltzed down to present-giving in that sexy little nightie, he'd been consumed with a desire so strong it had taken every ounce of his will-power to keep himself in check.

Her giving him that exquisite and very expensive miniature golf set had tormented him further, giving rise to the provocative possibility that, despite her new boyfriend, she still secretly fancied *him*. But her rather offhand words that her present was a parting gift of gratitude had propelled Nick back to cold, hard reality.

Sarah was well and truly over her school-girl crush on him. He'd lost his chance with her, if he'd ever had one.

It was this last thought that was bothering him the most.

'You should be glad she's over you,' he muttered as he marched towards the bathroom, stripping off his T-shirt as he went. 'Now all you have to do is concentrate on getting through today without behaving badly.'

Nick wrenched off his jeans, before walking over to snap on the water in the shower.

'No sarcastic remarks,' he lectured himself as he stepped under the ice-cold spray. 'No telling Derek you bought his girl-friend thirty-thousand-dollar earrings. And definitely no looking, no matter *what* she wears!'

CHAPTER SEVEN

'LET'S go, Sarah.'

Nick's loud command—called through her bedroom door—was accompanied by an impatient knocking.

Sarah's bedside clock showed it was three minutes to twelve, two minutes after Nick had asked her to be downstairs.

'Coming,' Sarah called back after one last nervous glance in her dressing-table mirror.

She did look good: the red and white sundress clung to her shapely but slender body, and her choice of hairstyle—she'd put it up—showed off her new diamond earrings.

It wasn't Sarah's sexy appearance that had the butterflies gathering in her stomach. It was this silly charade with Derek. Nick was going to spot something strange about their relationship, she felt sure of it!

But it was too late now. Derek was on his way, having texted her a while back to say the taxi he'd ordered had just arrived and he should be at her place by twelve.

Sarah pulled her scarlet-glossed mouth back into what she hoped passed for a happy smile and hurried across the room, movement setting her earrings swinging. When she wrenched open the door, Nick glanced up from where he was leaning with his back against the gallery railing. He still looked tired, she thought, but very handsome in fawn chinos and a brown and cream striped short-sleeved shirt.

'I'm ready,' she said breezily.

Nick's dark eyes swept over her from head to toe, his top lip curling slightly, as it did sometimes. 'Yes, but ready for what?'

His sarcasm rankled, as always.

Sarah planted her hands on her hips, just above where her skirt flared out saucily. 'It wouldn't hurt you to say something nice to me for a change.'

His eyebrows lifted, as though she'd surprised him with her stance. 'That's a matter of opinion. But if you insist…' His eyes travelled over her again, this time much more slowly.

A huge lump formed in her throat when his gaze lingered on her breasts before lifting to her mouth, then up to her eyes. If she'd been hoping to see desire in his detailed survey, however, she was doomed to disappointment.

'You look utterly gorgeous today, Sarah,' he said at last, but in a rather dry fashion. 'Derek is a very lucky man.'

Sarah was tempted to stamp her foot in frustration when the doorbell rang, saving her from her uncharacteristic temper tantrum.

'That'll probably be Derek now,' she tossed off instead, and bolted for the stairs, eager to answer the door without Nick being too close a witness to their greeting.

It wasn't Derek at the door, but an attractive, thirty-something brunette wearing a wrap-around electric-blue dress and a smile that would have cut glass.

Sarah knew immediately who it was.

'Sarah, I presume,' the woman said archly after a swift once-over that made her ice-blue eyes even icier. 'I'm Chloe, Nick's girl-friend.'

Of course you are, Sarah thought tartly. Nick's girlfriends might look different from one another—this one had a very short, chic hairdo, plus a much curvier body than the others. But underneath their varied physical features always lay a hard-nosed piece with no genuine warmth or niceness.

Sarah despised Chloe on sight.

'Hi there,' she managed politely before spinning round to see where Nick was. No way was she going to be caught having to make small talk with the bitch *du jour*.

Nick was still coming down the stairs, his expression none too happy.

'Chloe's here,' she called out to him.

For a split-second, Sarah could have sworn he had no idea who she was talking about. But then the penny dropped and he hurried to the door, his disgruntled face breaking into a smile.

'Happy Christmas, darling,' Chloe gushed as she threw herself into Nick's arms.

Sarah turned away so that she didn't have to watch them kiss, her stomach contracting when she heard Chloe whisper something about giving him his main Christmas present later that night.

It was extremely fortunate that Derek chose that moment to arrive, Sarah's nervous anticipation over their charade was obliterated in the face of her need to have someone by her side *on* her side.

'Derek, darling!' she gushed in much the same way Chloe had. 'Merry Christmas. Oh, it's so good to see you.' She let out a mental sigh of relief when she took in the way he was dressed. She'd been a bit worried he might wear a pink Paisley shirt, or something equally suspect. But no, he looked very attractive and sportily masculine in knee-length cargo shorts and a chest-hugging sky-blue top that complimented his fair colouring and showed off his great body.

'And you too, babe,' Derek returned, startling Sarah with his choice of endearment, not to mention his leaning over the rather large present he was holding to kiss her full on the mouth, taking his time.

'You look incredible,' he said on straightening. 'Doesn't she look incredible, everyone?'

Neither Nick nor Chloe said a word.

Sarah flushed with embarrassment, but Derek was undeterred.

'I hope this fits, babe,' he said, then pressed the present into her hands. 'I saw it in a shop window and I thought straight away that it was you to a T.'

Sarah didn't know whether to be pleased, or afraid of the contents. Derek had a wicked streak in him that was proving to be as entertaining as it was worrying.

'I...I'll open it a bit later,' she hedged. 'I have to help Nick greet our guests. Which reminds me. Nick, this is Derek,' she said by way of a formal introduction. 'Derek, this is Nick, my guardian.'

'No kidding,' Derek said as he shook Nick's hand. 'I got the impression you'd be older.'

Sarah tried not to laugh. But it was rather funny, seeing the expression on Nick's face.

'And I'm Chloe,' Chloe said with a sickeningly sweet smile. 'Nick's girlfriend.'

It never ceased to amaze Sarah how females like Chloe possessed split personalities—a super-sweet one for dealing with the male sex, a super-sour one, for their own.

'Why don't you go open your Christmas pressie in private?' Chloe suggested to Sarah with pretend saccharin-sweetness. 'I can help Nick answer the door, can't I, darling? I mean, all of the guests—other than Derek, of course—are Nick's friends.'

'What a good idea!' Sarah said, jumping at the chance to remove herself from Chloe's irritating presence. Of all Nick's girlfriends, she disliked this one the most, the conniving, two-faced cow!

'No, not down there,' Derek whispered when she grabbed his elbow and began steering him across the foyer towards the sunken family room. 'Take me upstairs. To your bedroom.'

'My *bedroom*!' she squawked, grinding to a halt.

'Ssh. Yes, your bedroom,' he went on softly. 'Don't ask why, just do it. And don't look back at either of those two. Just giggle, and then skip up those stairs with me.'

'I *never* giggle.' She hated females who giggled.

'You're going to today. That is, if you don't want to wonder for the rest of your life what it would be like to spend a night in Mr Dreamy's bed.'

Sarah finally saw what he was up to. 'This won't work, Derek, trust me.'

'No, you trust me. I know what I'm doing here, Sarah. I'm a master at the art of sexual jealousy. All gays are.'

'Ssh. Don't say that out loud.'

'Then do as you're told.'

Sarah refused to giggle. But she did laugh, then let Derek usher her with somewhat indecent speed up the stairs.

'Which room is yours?' he asked once they reached the landing.

'The third one on the right.'

'Nice room,' he said on closing the door behind them.

'Nick thinks it's too girlie. He also thinks I'm too thin now. He still doesn't fancy me, Derek. You're wasting your time trying to make him jealous.'

Derek smiled. 'That's not the impression I got when I kissed you.'

'What do you mean?'

'I kept my eyes open a fraction and watched your guardian's reaction over your shoulder.'

'And?'

'He hated it. And he hated me. I could feel his hatred hitting me in waves. Then, when he shook my hand he tried to crush my fingers.'

Sarah shook her head as she walked over and placed Derek's present on her pink quilt. 'I don't believe you,' she said as she sat down next to it.

'Why not?'

'Because I…Because he…Just because!' she snapped.

'You know what, Sarah? I think you're afraid.'

'Afraid of what?'

'Of success. You've lived with this fantasy for far too long. It's time to either let it go, or try to make it real. Which is it to be?'

Sarah thought of lying alone in this bed tonight whilst Nick cavorted with Chloe in his bed. She squeezed her eyes tightly shut for several seconds whilst she made up her mind. Then she opened them and looked into Derek's patiently waiting face.

'So what's the plan of action?'

Derek grinned. 'Stay right where we are, for starters. What time is lunch served?'

'Actually it's not served as such. It's a buffet. Nick usually tries to get everyone heading for the food at one o'clock.'

Derek glanced at his watch. 'In that case we'll make a reappearance downstairs at around five to one.'

Sarah frowned. 'We're going to stay up here till then?'

'Yep.'

'You do realise what Nick is going to think we're doing.'

'Yep.'

'He'll think I'm a slut!'

'If I'm right about him, he'll have trouble thinking at all. Now open your present. And make sure, when you come downstairs, you tell him what I gave you.'

CHAPTER EIGHT

NICK tried to hide his growing agitation, but where the hell was Sarah and what in God's name was she doing? It didn't take *that* long to open one miserable present. Damn it all, it was getting on for one o'clock.

The obvious answer just killed him: she was up in her bedroom, doing unspeakable things with that lounge lizard she was madly in love with and who had obviously pulled the wool over her eyes.

If ever Nick had seen a fortune-hunter it was darling Derek, with his fake smile, his fake blonde hair and his equally fake suntan!

Unfortunately his muscles didn't look fake, a fact that irritated the death out of Nick. He'd never thought Sarah was the sort of girl whose head could be turned by such superficial attractions. But clearly she was. She even seemed to like being called babe.

Didn't she know darling Derek probably called every one of his girlfriends babe? Saved him having to remember their names, since it was obvious he didn't have enough brains to make his head ache.

'Nick, Jeremy's talking to you,' Chloe said somewhat waspishly.

'What? Oh, sorry.' Nick dragged his mind away from his mental vitriol to focus back on the man talking to him.

Jeremy was his production company's location manager. Quite brilliant at his job, and gayer than gay.

'What were you saying, Jerry?'

Jeremy gave him a sunny smile over the rim of his martini. 'Just that I'm super-grateful to you for inviting *moi* for lunch today. Christmas is the one time of year when gays are severely reminded that lots of people are still homophobic. We try telling ourselves that Sydney is a very sophisticated city these days, but it's not as sophisticated as it pretends to be.'

'Really?' Nick said, his eyes returning to

the foyer through which Sarah would have to come. If she ever came back downstairs, that was.

'You'd think the world had more important things to worry about than what people do in their private lives, wouldn't you?' Jeremy rattled on. 'I mean…what business is it of others who or what you have sex with, as long as you're not hurting anyone?'

But what if you were? came Nick's savage thought. What if having sex with someone—right at this moment—was tearing someone else's insides out?

'Well said, Jeremy,' his partner complimented.

Nick's eyes swung to Kelvin, who was a tall, skinny fellow of indeterminate age.

Nick was about to open his mouth and make some possibly rude remark—he suspected he was on the verge of behaving very badly indeed—when the movement he'd been waiting for caught the corner of his eye.

Nick's guts crunched down hard as he watched the object of his agitation waltz across the foyer with a smug-looking Derek hot on her heels.

That Sarah's hair was down—and tousled—did not escape Nick. Neither did her flushed cheeks.

'If you'll excuse me,' he said abruptly, 'there's someone I must speak to. Chloe, could you show our guests out to the terrace? The lunch is a buffet, but there are place cards on the table.'

Nick ignored the flash of annoyance that zoomed across Chloe's face, just before he spun away and marched across the family room to confront Sarah. What he thought he was going to say he had no idea. But he needed to say something; anything to give vent to the storm of emotion building to a head within him.

'Sarah,' he bit out when he was close enough to the lovebirds.

Her eyes jerked round towards him.

'I need to talk to you. *Now.* In private.'

'But we were just going out to the terrace for lunch,' she returned, oh, so sweetly.

He gritted his teeth as his furious gaze fastened on her mouth, where her red lipstick was an even glossier red than it had been before. Courtesy, no doubt, of having had to be retouched.

But the *coup de grâce* to his already teetering control was noticing that she'd removed his diamond earrings.

'I'm sure you won't mind not eating for a further five minutes,' he snapped, his stomach turning over at the thought of why she wasn't still wearing his Christmas gift.

Her shrug seemed carefree, but he detected a smidgeon of worry in her eyes.

'I won't be long, darling,' she said to her lover with a softly apologetic stroke on his arm. 'The buffet's all set up on the terrace out there. You go ahead and I'll join you shortly.'

'Sure thing, babe. I'll choose for you. And get you some of that white wine you like.'

'Would you? That would be wonderful.'

The schmaltzy exchange almost made Nick sick to his stomach. The moment Derek departed he grabbed Sarah by the elbow and steered her back out to the foyer, then along the front hallway towards his study.

When she tried to wrench her arm free, his hand tightened its hold.

'Is this caveman stuff really necessary?' she protested.

Nick said nothing, just pushed her into his study, then banged the door shut behind them. When he glowered over her, she did look a little shamefaced.

'OK, you're mad at me for not coming downstairs earlier and helping you with your guests,' she said. 'That's it, isn't it?'

'Not only was your behaviour rude, Sarah, it was embarrassing.'

'Embarrassing! I don't see how. I mean, it's not as though I know any of the guests this year. Flora told me beforehand that all of them are from your production company.'

'That's no excuse for ignoring them,' he lashed out. 'They have heard me speak of you. They *expected* to meet you, but you were nowhere to be seen. On Christmas Day, of all days! It would have been polite of you to be in the family room, offering drinks and making conversation. Instead, you were upstairs in your bedroom, having sex with that obsequious boyfriend of yours.

I would have thought you had more pride, and a better sense of decorum.'

Her cheeks went bright red. 'Derek is not obsequious. And I was *not* having sex with him.'

Nick's laugh was both cold and contemptuous. 'Your appearance rather contradicts that.'

Her mouth fell open, then snapped shut. 'What Derek and I do in the privacy of my room is none of your business. Just as it's none of my business what you'll be doing with Chloe tonight in your bedroom. We're both adults now, Nick. I've been an adult for quite some time, in case you haven't noticed. In six weeks' time, I'll be twenty-five and you'll no longer have any say in my life whatsoever. I will be able to do whatever I like in this house because you won't be in it!'

'And no one will be more pleased than me,' he threw back at her, his frustration making him reckless. 'Do you think I've enjoyed being your bloody guardian? Do you think it's been fun, trying to keep you safe from all the sleazebags? Do you have any idea how hard it's been for me, keeping my own hands off you?'

There! He'd said it. It was out in the open now. His dark secret, his guilty obsession.

Nick hated the shock in her face. But it was a relief, in a way.

'You never guessed?' he said, his soul suddenly weary.

She shook her head. 'You...you never said anything.'

Nick's smile was wry. 'I owed it to Ray to do what he asked me to do.'

'He asked you to keep away from me?'

'He asked me to protect you from the scoundrels of this world.'

If anything, this statement shocked her more than his admitting his desire.

'But you're not a scoundrel!'

'Trust me, Sarah. I'm a scoundrel of the first order. Always was. Always will be. Believe me, if you were any other man's daughter I would have seduced you when I had the chance. Because I did have a chance with you, didn't I? When you were sixteen.'

'You mean when I kissed you that time? You actually wanted me back then?'

'That's putting it mildly. Don't imagine for a single moment that I was worried about your age. Such things have never mattered to me. I just couldn't bear the thought that the one man in the world whom I liked and respected might look at me with disgust. Ray's words of praise and acceptance meant more to me than my intense but inconvenient desire for you.'

'I…I see…'

Nick doubted it. How could someone as basically sweet and naïve as Sarah understand the dark and damaged undercurrents of his character?

'Go on. Go back to your Derek,' he commanded.

'He…he's not my Derek.'

'What? What do you mean by that?'

'Derek's not my lover. He's just a friend. He's also gay.'

'*Gay!*' Nick repeated, his mind whirling as he tried to make sense of Sarah's confession.

'You've just been brutally honest with me, so I'm going to be brutally honest with you. I brought Derek to today's lunch so that I wouldn't be alone. And hopefully, to make you jealous.'

Nick stared at her.

Sarah looked as if she was about to cry. 'I've had a crush on you for as long as I can remember,' she blurted out.

Nick grimaced. He hated that word, crush. It sound so schoolgirlish. Of course, Sarah was still very young, compared to him. He'd been old from the time he was thirteen.

'You still have a chance with me, Nick,' she went on, her green eyes glistening. 'If you want it…'

If he wanted it. Dear God, if she only knew.

But what he wanted bore no resemblance to what she wanted.

'I'm no good for you, Sarah,' he bit out, surprising himself that he could find the will-power to resist what she was foolishly offering him.

'Why not?' she demanded to know.

'You know why not. I hid nothing from you when you were a youngster. I told you more than once: I can't fall in love.'

'I'm not asking you to.'

He glowered at her. 'Don't you dare lower yourself in that fashion. Don't you dare! I know you, Sarah. You want love and marriage and children. You do not want some decadent affair with a man of little conscience and even less moral fibre.'

'So you're knocking me back again. Is that the bottom line?'

'I already have a girlfriend,' he said coldly. 'I don't need you.'

The hurt in her eyes showed Nick that he'd done the right thing. Sarah's crush would have deepened into love if he slept with her. It had happened to him before, which was why he always stuck to partners like Chloe these days.

But that didn't mean he felt good about rejecting Sarah. His body was already regretting it.

'You'll find Mr Right one day,' he said stiffly.

'Oh, don't be so bloody pompous,' she snapped at him. 'If I wanted Mr Right, do you think I'd have just propositioned *you*? But that's all right, there are plenty of other good-looking studs around. Once I inherit all Daddy's lovely money, I don't think I'll be wanting for lovers, do you? Now I'm going to go eat my Christmas lunch. You can please yourself with what you do!'

CHAPTER NINE

'DOES that face mean good news or bad news?' Derek asked after Sarah had dragged the chair out next to him, and plonked herself down.

'Don't talk to me just yet. I'm so mad I could spit.'

'Oooh. I wish I'd been a fly on the wall. Here, have some wine. It's a very good Chardonnay from the Hunter Valley.'

'I don't give a damn what it is as long as it's alcohol.'

Sarah lifted the glass to her lips and swallowed deep and hard.

'I hope you like seafood,' Derek said, indicating the plateful he'd collected for her.

'At this point in time, I like anything which is edible. And drinkable!'

Sarah could still hardly believe what had

just happened. Her fantasy man had confessed that he fancied her. Had claimed he'd fancied her way back when she'd been fifteen!

She'd been within a hair's breadth of having her most longed-for dream come true and what had he done? Rejected her, in favour of the brown-haired witch sitting two chairs down from her.

'Sarah!' the witch suddenly snapped. 'Where on earth is Nick? I got his meal for him and now he's not here to eat it.'

Sarah gained some pleasure from seeing that Chloe was not pleased with her lover's absence. Not pleased at all!

'I have absolutely no idea where he is,' came her seemingly nonchalant reply, which was followed up by another large gulp of wine.

'But weren't you just talking to him?'

'Yes,' she replied airily.

The witch's eyes narrowed. 'So what were you two talking about? Or weren't you talking at all?'

Sarah blinked, her wine glass stilling in mid-air. 'What?'

'You don't fool me,' Chloe spat. 'I know what's going on here with you and Nick. I knew it the moment I clapped eyes on you.'

'Knew what, Chloe?'

Both Sarah and Chloe jumped at Nick's reappearance, Sarah quite stunned by the ice in his voice. And his eyes.

Chloe's own eyes stayed hard. 'Don't take me for a fool, Nick. I know jealousy when I see it. And I know you. No way could you have lived all these years with a girl of Sarah's—shall we say?—attractions—without sampling them for yourself. '

Sarah's mouth gaped open whilst Nick's hands tightened over the back of his chair, his knuckles going white. 'Are you accusing me of sleeping with my ward?'

'For want of a better word—yes.'

Sarah suddenly became aware that a silence had fallen over the long, trestle-style table. In the distance she could hear the sound of a speedboat on the harbour. Up close, all she could hear was her own heart beating loudly in her chest.

'If that's what you think,' Nick said, 'then I suggest you leave.'

Chloe looked rattled for a moment, but only for a moment. Her face became a sour mask as she scraped her chair back and stood up. 'I couldn't agree more. I'm not a girl who tolerates being cheated on.'

'I never cheated on you,' Nick stated curtly.

'If that's so, then it's only because Sarah decided she temporarily preferred Derek to you. I am well aware she hasn't been home lately. But be warned, Derek,' she flung in Derek's direction, 'she belonged to Nick first. Isn't that right, Sarah?'

Sarah could have lied. But she wanted this creature gone from Nick's life.

'Yes, that's right,' she said, and there was a immediate buzz around the table. Chloe's face showed a savage satisfaction, whilst Nick's expression carried alarm.

'But not the way you're implying,' Sarah went on, determined not to let this witch-woman ruin Nick's reputation in the eyes of his business colleagues. 'Nick has always had my love, and he always will. He has not, however, ever acted in any way with me but as my protector, and my friend. So yes, I agree with Nick. If you believe he's behaved in such a dishonourable fashion, then you should leave. There is no place in my home for anyone who doesn't hold Nick in the same high regard in which my father did, and in which I do. So please,' she said, and stood up also, 'let me show you to the door.'

'No,' Nick said, and pressed a gentle but firm hand on her shoulder. 'Let me.'

Sarah threw him a grateful glance before sinking back down into her chair, only then realising her knees were very wobbly indeed.

'Good luck,' Chloe grated out with one last vicious look at Sarah. 'You're going to need it.'

As Nick shepherded Chloe from the terrace, Derek began a slow clap, joined by several of the guests.

'Very impressive, sweetie,' Derek said softly. 'But also rather telling.'

Sarah's head jerked around towards him. 'In what way?'

'Blind Freddie can see you're in love with the man.'

Sarah sighed. 'Was I that obvious?'

'Afraid so.'

'Oh, dear.'

'No matter. Now, tell me what happened a little while back that made you so mad. Was Nick as jealous as Chloe said he was?'

'Yes.'

'I *knew* it! He fancies you, doesn't he?'

Sarah shook her head. 'I couldn't believe it when he told me he did. And not just lately. Since I was sixteen.'

'Wow. Did you tell him you fancied him right back?'

'Yes.'

Derek looked confused. 'Then I don't get it. What's the problem? Not me, I hope. You did tell him I wasn't your real boyfriend, didn't you?'

'Oh, yes. I was totally honest with him. I even told him you were gay.'

'*And?*'

'He still rejected me. Said he was no good for me.'

'*What?*'

'He told me my father asked him to protect me from the scoundrels of this world, of which he rates himself the gold-medal winner.'

'For crying out loud, can't the man see

that his not sleeping with you all these years makes him one of the good guys?'

'Obviously not.'

'This calls for even sneakier action. Now, tonight I suggest you—'

'Stop, Derek,' she broke in. 'Just stop.'

'You're giving up,' he said, disappointment in his voice.

'No, I'm moving on. And so is Nick. He's already told me he can't wait to leave here.'

'That's because he can't trust himself around you. You've got him on the ropes, sweetie, and he's running for cover.'

'Then let him run. It's over, Derek.'

'How can it be over when it hasn't even begun?'

'Could we just leave this conversation and eat?'

Derek shrugged, then fell to devouring some prawns.

Sarah was doing her best to force some food down her throat when Nick returned to the table. Her hand tightened around her fork whilst he removed Chloe's chair, along with her plate, before pulling out his own chair and reseating himself.

'Sorry about that, Sarah,' he muttered as he shook out his serviette. 'Thank you for standing up for me.'

'That's all right. Chloe shouldn't have said what she did.'

'No, she shouldn't have. But I can understand why she did. Jealousy can make you do…stupid things.'

'Yes, I know. I'm truly sorry for this whole charade today, Nick.'

'I wasn't talking about you, Sarah. I was talking about myself.'

Her head turned and their eyes connected.

'You *were* jealous, weren't you?' she whispered.

'We're not going to go there again, Sarah,' he warned her abruptly. 'Do I make myself clear?'

If his harsh voice wasn't sufficiently convincing, his cold eyes were.

'Crystal clear,' she said.

'Good. Now let's forget about everything that has happened today so far and enjoy our Christmas lunch.'

Sarah sat there in stunned silence when Nick tucked into his food with apparent relish. She was even more amazed when he started up a very lively conversation with the man on his immediate right.

Was he just pretending, or hadn't he been genuinely upset by the events of the day? Chloe had been his girlfriend for the last six months and she'd just been dismissed in an instant.

Hadn't he cared about her at all?

Obviously not.

Maybe Nick was right. Maybe he was a scoundrel.

Sarah slid her eyes to her right, where she surreptitiously watched him eat half a dozen oysters; watched him lift each oyster shell to his lips, tip his head back, then slide the tasty morsel down his throat, after which he would lick his lips with relish.

Sarah finally found herself echoing this action with her own tongue, moving it over her suddenly parched lips, her heartbeat quickening when his head turned her way.

He stared at her wet lips for a long moment, before his mouth pulled back into a twisted smile. 'You just can't stop, can you?'

'Stop what?' she choked out.

'The tempting. No, don't bother to deny it. Or defend yourself. Everything you've done today has been leading to this moment. Very well. You've won. Though I doubt you'll see it as a win by tomorrow morning.'

'What do you mean?'

Again, that cold, cryptic smile. 'I did warn you. If you insist on playing with the devil, then you have to be prepared to take the consequences.'

CHAPTER TEN

THE rest of the afternoon was endless, an eternity of wondering and worrying exactly what Nick meant by his provocative yet threatening words.

Several times Sarah tried to draw him into further clarification but he would have none of it, always turning the conversation away from the subject, or turning away from her altogether. After the lunch was over he deserted her to play the role of host, mingling with all his guests and making sure they had a good time. Coffee was served around the pool, with a few of the guests changing afterwards for a swim. Unfortunately Nick joined them, the sight of him in his brief black costume not doing Sarah's agitated state of mind any good.

It was around this time that Derek received

a call on his cellphone from his mother, saying that his father had had a change of heart and wanted him to come home for Christmas after all. A delighted Derek called a taxi straight away and rushed off, leaving Sarah pleased for him, but even more lonely and agitated herself. In desperation, she left the party and escaped to the privacy of her bedroom.

But there was no peace for her there. She could still hear the gaiety downstairs through the French doors, the sounds tormenting her. What kind of man was Nick to say what he'd said to her and then ignore her? Finally, she could not bear her solitude any longer and made her way out onto the balcony, where she had a perfect view of the pool below…and Nick.

He saw her watching him, she knew. But he still ignored her, choosing instead to put his head down and swim, up and down, up and down. He must have swum for a good fifteen minutes straight before he stopped abruptly at one end and hauled himself out of the pool. Grabbing a towel, he draped it around his dripping shoulders before throwing her a savage glance, then striding up the terrace steps and disappearing under the roof created by the canvas blinds.

Every female nerve-ending in Sarah's body went on high alert. He was coming upstairs. To change? Or for something else?

She gripped the wrought-iron railing of the balcony, hot blood rushing around her veins at the possibility that it was *her* he was coming for; that he was about to put his teasing words into action. It didn't seem possible that he would do such a thing with the house still full of guests. But he'd said he was a scoundrel, hadn't he?

Sarah did not hear him enter her bedroom. But she felt his presence in every pore of her body. She whirled to find him standing in the doorway that led out onto the balcony. The towel was no longer draped around his shoulders. His legs were set solidly apart, his hands balled into fists by his sides.

Sarah had seen him dressed in nothing but his swimming costume many times, but never in her bedroom, and never with that look on his face.

She shivered under the impact of the dark passion emanating from his coal-black eyes.

'Come here,' he commanded, his voice low and harsh.

Shock—and a sudden wave of fear—held her motionless.

He stunned her further by stripping down to total nudity, leaving her to confront the physical evidence of his desire.

Now, *that* she'd never seen before, and a dark excitement sent her head spinning and her pulse racing.

'Come here,' he repeated in gravelly tones.

She moved across the balcony like some robot, her mouth dry, her heart thudding loudly behind her ribs. When she was close enough he reached up to cup her heated face, his eyes holding hers captive whilst his mouth lowered to her still parched lips.

But he didn't kiss her. He just slowly licked her lips with his tongue. She found it incredibly erotic, her eyes shutting as her lips fell further apart on a soft moan.

Another moan punched from Sarah's throat when his tongue suddenly slid into her mouth. Surprise swiftly gave way to a wild craving to draw him in deeper and yet deeper. The need to pleasure him was great; the need to possess him even greater.

Her eyes flung wide when he wrenched his tongue away, her cry the cry of dismay. But then his hands fell to her shoulders and he was pushing her down onto her knees in front of him.

Any shock was momentary. If this was what he wanted, then she wanted it too.

He tasted clean and salty from the swimming pool. But it wasn't the taste of him that mattered to Sarah. All the years of wanting him to want her made her both reckless and wild. Her secret passion was finally unleashed.

Afterwards, she had no detailed recollection of how long it was before he came. A minute perhaps. Maybe two.

All she could recall was her satisfaction in his release, thrilling to the raw groans that filled the room, exulting in his uncontrolled surrender.

She glanced up at him, still unbearably aroused by what she'd just done. Her body was on fire, her conscience in danger of being totally routed. She did not care if he was a scoundrel. Did not care if he was only using her. She'd never been so excited in all her life.

'You do realise there's no going back now,' he grated out as he lifted her to her feet.

She just stared at him, unable to formulate any reply at that moment.

He stared back with hard, glittering eyes. 'I should have known you'd do this to me today.'

'Do what?' she choked out.

'Make me cross the line. You think you know what you're doing but you don't.'

'I'm not a child, Nick.'

He laughed. 'You are, compared to me. But that's all right. That's your attraction. I like it that you're relatively innocent. It excites me. It'll almost be worth it to open your eyes, to make you see what kind of men there are in this world. And how easily it is for them to seduce girls like you. Hopefully, by the time I've finished with you, you'll have enough experience to protect yourself in future.'

'I'm not that innocent,' she threw back at him.

'No? Why do you say that? Because you think you know how to go down on a man?'

Sarah's face flamed.

'I'm not saying that I didn't enjoy it,' Nick went on, reaching out to stroke a perversely loving hand down her cheek. 'But I'll enjoy teaching you how to do it properly a lot more.'

His hand drifted across to her mouth, where he inserted a finger between her lips.

'Most men prefer not to be gobbled up like fast food,' he advised, sliding that knowing finger back and forth along the middle of her tongue. 'Once you master the art, you can love a man more times than you would think possible. Have you ever been made love to all night long, Sarah?'

A shudder rippled down Sarah's spine at the images he was evoking.

'I think not,' he purred, his dark gaze narrowing on her wide eyes.

His finger retreated, leaving her feeling weirdly bereft and empty.

'But tonight you will, my love,' he

promised. 'Tonight, I will take you to places you've never been before. If that's what you want, of course. Do you want it, Sarah? This is your last chance to tell me to go to hell.'

She stared into his heavily lidded eyes, afraid now of the power he had over her.

But her fear was not as strong as her desire.

'So be it,' he snapped when she said nothing. 'Just remember that you must live with the consequences of your decision.'

'What consequences?'

'That one day, I will have had my fill of you and you will go the way of all the others,' he said so coldly it was scary.

'Are you trying to frighten me off?'

His laugh was hard, and lacking in humour. 'Good God, no. I want nothing more than to have that gorgeous body of yours at my daily disposal till at least the end of the summer holidays. But I have a policy of brutal honesty with all my girlfriends. Chloe knew the score. Now you do too.'

'Can I tell Flora that I'm your new girl-friend?'

His face darkened at this suggestion. 'Absolutely not!'

'I thought that might be the case. You want to keep me your dirty little secret, don't you?'

'I do have my pride. Don't you?' he threw at her challengingly.

Her chin lifted. 'Yes.'

'Then it will be *our* dirty little secret. If you're not happy with that, then we can still call it quits. Right now. After all, one swallow doesn't make a summer.'

Sarah sucked in sharply at this most outrageous *double entendre*. 'You really are a wicked devil, aren't you?'

'I did warn you about my character. So what's your final decision? I can leave you and this house asap. Or…' He walked over to the bed, where Derek's present was lying spread out on the pink quilt. It was a black satin and lace teddy, which left little to the imagination, bought with the idea of making Nick jealous.

He picked it up, his eyebrows arching as he turned it this way and that. 'Or you can agree to come to my bedroom tonight, wearing nothing but this and my diamond earrings.'

Sarah tried to feel disgusted with him, and herself. But it was no use. There was no room in her quivering body at that moment for anything but a wild rush of dizzying excitement. She could not wait to do what he asked, could not wait to present herself to him the way he asked.

What did that make her?

A masochist, or just a girl in love, a girl who'd lived for far too long with her romantic fantasies.

Yet he wasn't offering her romance, just a few weeks of the kind of lovemaking she hadn't experienced before. He was right about that. All her lovers so far had been youngish men of little *savoir-faire*.

But the way Nick was talking made her wonder if there were ways nice girls didn't know about.

The thought only excited her further.

'What time tonight?' she asked, and looked him straight in the eye.

No way was she going to let him think he'd seduced her into this. She would come to him willingly, with courage, not fear.

His smile was wry. 'I've always known

you had spirit, Sarah. That's another of your many attractions. Shall we say nine? Flora and Jim will have retired to their quarters by then.'

'Nine,' she repeated in pained tones. That was over four hours away!

'Yes, I know. But it will be all the better for the waiting. Now I must go and dress,' he said, bending to snatch up his swimming costume and towel from where they lay on the cream carpet. 'Meanwhile I suggest you go downstairs. People might begin to wonder where we are, and jump to the conclusion that there's some truth in Chloe's accusations. Just don't forget to replenish your lipstick before you go.'

Sarah stared after him as he left. Then she whirled and hurried into the bathroom.

CHAPTER ELEVEN

'I KNEW Chloe had just about reached her use-by date,' Flora remarked as she packed the dishwasher for the last time that evening. 'But I still can't believe Nick broke up with her on Christmas Day.'

Sarah glanced up from where she was sitting, having a cup of coffee. The clock on the wall showed twenty-two minutes past eight.

'He's a right devil with women,' Flora rattled on, 'but I've never thought of him as cruel.'

Strangely enough, Sarah agreed with Flora.

'He really had no option after Chloe accused him of carrying on with me in front of everyone,' she defended.

Flora pulled a face. 'I suppose not. I just

wish I'd been there. Trust something exciting to happen the first year Jim and I decide to eat Christmas dinner back in our rooms. So tell me, what led up to it?'

Sarah shrugged. 'I have no idea. One minute everything seemed fine, the next she just came out with it. We were both shocked, I can tell you.'

'I'll bet it was because of the way you look today. She was probably blind with jealousy.'

'That's what Nick said.'

'He'd have been furious with her for saying something like that in front of his work colleagues. But I heard you set her to rights.'

'Really? Who told you that?' She'd done her best not to provide Flora with too many details, in case she slipped up with her story.

'One of the waiters. He said it was the most interesting Christmas lunch they'd ever catered for.'

'It was darned embarrassing. I'm glad it's over. Next year, things are going to be very different.'

Sarah wished she hadn't said that. Because she didn't want to think about next year. She didn't want to think about anything but tonight.

But once the thought was put in her head, it was impossible to banish it. If Nick had been telling the truth earlier, then by next Christmas she would be long gone from his life, and from his bed.

'You won't change your mind?' Flora asked.

'About what?'

'About letting me cook a hot meal next year. Call me old-fashioned, but Christmas just doesn't feel like Christmas without a turkey and a plum pudding. I know Nick won't mind. He really likes turkey.'

'Nick probably won't be here,' Sarah said a bit stiffly.

'What? Why not?'

'He's moving out in February.'

'So what? You'll invite him here for Christmas, surely. You and he are like family.'

'He might not want to come.'

'Rubbish! He loves having Christmas here. Even when he was building that resort on Happy Island, he always came back for

Christmas. And it's not as though he'll go off and get married and make a home of his own.'

'True,' Sarah agreed ruefully, her eyes dropping to her coffee. 'That's never going to happen.'

So don't start secretly hoping that it will. He's not going to fall in love with you, no matter how much you love him. You're just another sexual partner, a temporary object of desire, a source of physical pleasure.

And when that pleasure begins to wane, when boredom sets in, you'll be replaced. That's the way it's always been with Nick and that's the way it will continue.

It might have been a seriously depressing train of thought if she'd been in a sensible, looking-after-her-future-happiness mood. But Sarah was anything but sensible at that moment. Excitement was fizzing through her veins, her insides wound so tight she was having trouble swallowing her coffee. How she managed to appear so composed in front of Flora, she had no idea. Obviously, she had the makings of an Oscar-winning actress!

'Where is Nick, by the way?' Flora asked.

'He went upstairs a little while ago,' Sarah replied as cool as you please. 'He said he was tired.'

'You finished with that?' Flora reached out for her coffee-mug.

Sarah handed it to her. 'I think I'll go up to bed, too,' she said, this time with a slight catch in her voice. 'It's been a long day.'

'There's a good movie on at eight-thirty,' Flora said. 'Got that film-star fellow in it that I like. Sexy devil. Now, he can put his slippers under my bed any time he likes.'

'Mmm,' Sarah murmured as she slid from the stool. Not as sexy as the devil she was about to spend the night with. 'Goodnight, Flora. Don't worry about breakfast. I'm going to sleep in. You should too. You look tired.'

'I am a bit. What about Nick?'

'I'll tell him to get himself something in the morning. I doubt he's asleep yet.'

'Before you go, Sarah, I just want to say how lovely you looked today. I wouldn't mind betting that by next Christmas you'll have a real boyfriend sitting at the Christmas table. Or even a fiancé. Which reminds me, did anything further develop with Derek today?'

'Er—no. He's not interested in me in that way.'

'What a pity. Still, there are plenty of other fish in the sea. Off you go, then.'

'Goodnight, Flora. Enjoy the movie.'

'Oh, I will.'

Sarah's pretend composure began to disintegrate the moment she left the kitchen.

'What on earth do you think you're doing?' she muttered to herself as she walked up the stairs on suddenly shaky legs. 'He's going to break your heart. You know that, don't you?'

Sarah stopped in front of his bedroom door. She even lifted her hand to knock. What she was going to say to him, she had no idea, though *go to hell* came to mind.

But then she heard the sound of Nick's shower running.

He was getting ready for her.

She could picture him standing naked under the jets of warm water, washing himself clean with long, soapy strokes of a sponge. In her mind's eye, he was already wanting her.

It was the thought of his wanting her that was the most corrupting. She'd wanted him to want her like this for years.

Impossible to turn her back on his desire.

Impossible to ignore her own.

Sarah's hand fell back to her side and she stumbled on to her bedroom.

Nick stood under the lukewarm spray, his hands braced against the shower-stall tiles, his eyes down.

Half an hour to go and already he was in agony.

Gritting his teeth, he turned the water to cold. Ten minutes later, he had his flesh under control again. But not his mind.

You should not be doing this, Nick, came the reproachful thought. She's in love with you. Or she thinks she is.

'You're a total bastard,' he growled to himself.

His mouth twisted into a sneer as he emerged from the shower stall and snatched up a towel. 'So what's new, Nick?'

Still, he *had* given her every chance to escape. She'd been right when she'd accused him of trying to frighten her off. He'd honestly thought when he pushed her to her knees the way he had that she would jump up and run a mile. But she hadn't...

Of course, his desire for Sarah had been building in his head for years. It was no wonder he'd found it difficult to control himself this afternoon.

Still, it was a worry, his lack of control. From the moment she'd taken him into her mouth, he'd just lost it. Totally.

As he stared at his reflection in the bathroom mirror, Nick vowed that tonight would be different. Tonight he would be the coolly confident lover he usually was, patiently taking her on an erotic journey that initially might feel romantic to a girl as young and naïve as she was.

By morning, however, she would see him for what he really was: a cold-blooded and ruthless bastard who used women for nothing but his own pleasure and satisfaction. She would see that any finer feelings would be wasted on him, at the same time becoming a lot wiser to the wicked ways of the world, and of men.

It was a perverse way to protect her, but then, he'd always been perverse when it came to Sarah. Hadn't he lusted after her when she'd been little more than a girl? A lust which had been as obsessive as it was unwanted.

This moment had been inevitable, Nick conceded as he finished drying himself. The only surprise was that he'd held back as long as he had.

Nine o'clock saw Sarah once again at Nick's door, her hands curling into white-knuckled balls as she struggled to find the courage to knock.

The black teddy fitted her perfectly, the skin-tight mid-section outlining her newly defined waist, the built-in lace bra cut low. More transparent lace inserts covered her hips, making the already high-cut sides seem even higher. But it was the back of the teddy that shocked her, mostly because there wasn't much of it. A couple of inches of material above her waist and next to nothing below, where it narrowed into a satin thong.

The door suddenly being wrenched open brought a gasp to her lips. Nick stood there, a dark red towel slung low around his hips, the expression on his face not a particularly happy one.

But his eyes changed as they swept over her, that white-hot desire she'd always wanted to see making her stomach flip right over.

'I knew you'd look beautiful in that. I didn't realise just how beautiful. And how damned sexy.'

He looked pretty damned sexy himself, she thought breathlessly.

His sudden frown worried her, as did his ragged sigh. 'You've made my life really difficult, Sarah.'

'No more than you've made mine,' she countered. Quite bravely, considering she was quaking inside.

He shook his head as he took her right hand in his and pulled her into the bedroom, kicking the door shut behind them.

'I presume you haven't changed your mind,' he said drily as he drew her across the room towards the bed.

'If I had, I wouldn't be wearing this, would I?' she threw at him with more feigned boldness whilst her gaze flicked nervously around.

She noted the bed, its red quilt thrown back, the black satin sheets glowing under the soft light of the red lampshades.

His suddenly scooping her up into his arms shattered her brave façade.

'You're trembling,' he said.

'Am I?'

'Very definitely.' He sighed for the second time, his eyes shutting for a moment. 'What am I going to do with you?'

'Make love to me, I hope. All night long, you promised.'

His eyes flicked open to glower down at her.

'No, Sarah. That's not what's going to happen here.'

Her heart plummeted to the floor.

'What I'm going to do is have sex with you. Don't mistake it for lovemaking. I never make love. I have sex with women. Of course,' he added with a sardonic smile as he lowered her gently into the middle of the bed, 'it will be great sex.'

Relief—and a rush of excitement—flooded through Sarah as her head and shoulders came to rest against the pile of satin-covered pillows. At this moment, he could call it whatever he liked. Nothing he could say would deter her from seeing this through.

But for Sarah, it would be lovemaking. For her, this was going to be the night of her life!

The satin sheets felt cool against her heated skin. Nick's eyes were cool as well, that white-hot desire she'd spotted earlier now not in evidence.

'Relax,' he advised as he straightened.

'I...I guess I am a bit nervous,' she admitted when he joined her on the bed.

'Yes, I can see that.'

Propping himself up on his side, he ran a teasing fingertip around the edge of the low-cut neckline, making her skin break out into goose-pimples. When he traced the neckline a second time, almost touching one of her nipples, she sucked in, then held her breath.

'Do you have extra-sensitive breasts?'

His question rattled her. Actually his

talking rattled her. None of her previous lovers had talked. They'd simply got on with it.

Sarah finally let go of her long-held breath. 'I...I don't know,' she said, her head spinning.

'Let's see, shall we?'

Sarah held her breath again as he levered the satin straps off her shoulders and peeled them slowly downwards till the lace cups gave up their prizes.

'Mmm. Delicious,' he said, and bent to lick her right nipple.

Sarah clenched her teeth hard in her jaw, lest she cry out. But oh, the dizzying pleasure of it.

When he drew her nipple into his mouth, she could not prevent a moan escaping.

When he nibbled at it with his teeth, she squirmed and whimpered.

His head lifted, his eyes glittering now.

'As much as this teddy looks fantastic on you, right at this moment I prefer you without it.'

Sarah gulped but said nothing as he peeled it down her body and off her feet before tossing it carelessly aside. His eyes were like laser beams, honing in on that private part of her body.

'I love looking at you,' he rasped, caressing her smooth pubic bone before sliding his fingers through the already damp folds of her sex.

'Oh,' Sarah choked out, stunned by the sensations that came crashing through her.

'You are so beautiful,' he crooned as he continued to explore her down there, touching her everywhere. Inside, outside, then inside again. More deeply this time, finding erotic zones she didn't know she had. She pressed herself urgently against his hand, her head twisting from side to side, her wide eyes pleading with his as her body raced towards a climax.

'It's OK,' he said, his voice rough, his eyelids heavy. 'I want to watch you come.'

Sexy words, sexy eyes. Pushing her over the edge in a free-fall of pleasure that was wonderfully wanton, till she came to earth with a thud and realised this was *not* what she'd waited a lifetime to experience: Nick watching her come.

But no sooner did these rather dismaying thoughts flash through her mind than he was kissing her, not wildly but gently, his mouth sipping softly at hers.

'Don't be upset,' he murmured between kisses. 'You needed that. You were wound too tight. Next time…I'll be inside you… and it'll be much better.'

She blinked up at him when his head rose.

The corner of his mouth lifted in a quirky smile. 'You don't believe me?'

'Oh, no,' she said truthfully, 'I believe you.'

'Then what is it?'

'I…I'm sorry, but I thought…before we go any further, what…what about protection? I mean…Oh, you know what I mean,' she said, annoyed with herself for stuttering and stammering. 'You've been around.'

His expression carried an element of reproach. 'Sarah, you don't honestly think I would risk making you pregnant, do you?'

'Well, actually, you can't,' she admitted. 'Make me pregnant, I mean. I'm on the Pill.'

'I see. But you still want me to use condoms?'

'I'm not a total fool, Nick.' Even if he thought she was for being here with him.

'You've no need to worry. I've got that taken care of. Relax. No way are you getting out of here, sweetheart. Not till your old Uncle Nick lets you.'

'Don't call yourself that!' she snapped as she struggled to suppress an involuntary moan. Dear heaven, but he was good at that. 'There's nothing wrong with our being together,' she threw at him in desperation.

'That depends on your definition of wrong,' he countered, his devastatingly knowing fingers not missing a beat as he touched her breasts again. 'But no matter. It's like I said this afternoon,' he went on, that knowing hand sliding slowly down over her stomach and back between her legs. 'I'd reached the point of no return.'

'I…I think I'm just about reaching it again, too,' she choked out.

'So soon?'

She squirmed against his hand, her still sensitised flesh unable to bear too much more.

'You have to stop that,' she cried.

He stopped, leaving her panting whilst he rolled away and yanked open the top drawer of his bedside table. He selected a condom and drew it on. When he returned to her body, he did not rush. Neither did he attempt any kind of weird or wonderful position, for which she was grateful. Sarah wanted to look into his face when he was inside her; wanted to hold him and love him as she'd always wanted to.

She tried not to cry out when he finally entered her. But she couldn't quite manage to contain herself, a raw sound escaping her throat. Do not fall apart, for pity's sake, she lectured herself. But there was a great lump in her throat and tears were threatening.

Nick's concern was instantaneous. 'Are you all right?' he asked, smoothing her hair back from her face and staring deep into her by then glistening eyes. 'I'm not hurting you, am I?'

What an ironic thing to say!

'No, no, I'm fine,' she insisted, though her voice sounded artificially high. 'Would you mind kissing me, please? I like to be kissed a lot.' Anything to stop him staring down at her in that thoughtful fashion.

'My pleasure,' he said, and lowered his mouth to hers.

It was a kiss that might have been the kiss of true love, if she hadn't known differently.

How hungry it was, how passionate… how heartbreaking.

When his body began to move in tandem with his tongue, her fragile emotions were forgotten as the physical experience took over. With each surge of his flesh she could feel the coil of desire tighten within her. It was exciting, yet frustrating at the same time. She wanted to come. But as the seconds turned into minutes there was no release for her, only an all-consuming heat that flooded her body and quickened her heartbeat to a point where her mouth was forced to burst away from his.

'Help me, Nick,' she sobbed as she dragged in some life-saving breaths.

'Look at me,' he commanded, cupping her face and stilling his flesh inside her.

She stared up at him, her eyes wide and wild, her mouth panting heavily.

'Wrap your legs higher around my back,' he advised. 'Then move *with* me. Lift your hips as I push forward, then lower them when I withdraw. There's no hurry, Sarah. Just look into my eyes and trust me.'

Just look into my eyes...

She never wanted to look anywhere else.

Trust me...

Oh, God. How she wanted to do that too.

This is all a big mistake, Nick thought as she blindly followed his instructions. How long had it been since he'd been so damned nice and considerate in bed?

Who was this Nick who was suddenly caring so much?

He didn't approve of him. Couldn't trust him. He might start thinking he'd changed.

Which was impossible. He was what he was and he'd never change. This was just a momentary aberration. He'd get over it.

The trouble was he didn't think he'd get over it in one night.

He began moving faster, and so did she, her eyes growing wider and more desperate-looking.

Her first spasm was so strong Nick almost came then and there, but he held on, watching with wonder as her face became suffused with a seductive mixture of surprise and sheer joy. He'd never seen a woman look like that before. Never felt a woman who felt the way she did, either.

Finally he surrendered his control, astonished at the intensity of his own climax, and the strange lurch to his heart when she pulled him down on top of her.

'Oh, Nick,' she cried, and nuzzled into his neck. 'Oh, my darling…'

Nick didn't say a word. He couldn't.

He'd never felt so confused. All he was sure of was that he'd never felt what he'd felt just now when she'd called him her darling. The endearment had wrenched at his very soul, that soul which he'd always imagined was too dark for such sentiment.

As he lay there with her cuddled up to him, Nick gradually became sure of something else: he didn't want to frighten Sarah off any more.

Which rather changed his plans for the rest of the night.

Nick didn't delude himself that this more

romantic side he'd unexpectedly discovered within himself would last. But, for now, he found it quite irresistible. He could not wait to make love to Sarah again, could not wait to see the delight in her eyes.

But first, there was something he had to do. Carefully he disentangled himself from her arms and headed for the bathroom, where he washed himself fresh and clean then returned to the bed. He was about to stir her with some kisses when the phone next to his bed began to ring.

CHAPTER TWELVE

SARAH woke to the sound of a phone ringing. For a split-second she had no idea where she was. But the feel of Nick's naked body pressed up against hers swiftly cleared the haze in her head, everything coming back in a rapid series of flashbacks.

Her, coming to his bedroom wearing that outrageous teddy.

Him, carrying her to the bed.

Her, lying back against these satin pillows.

Him, making love to her.

But then came another memory: she'd called him darling afterwards.

When the phone continued to ring, Nick sighed then rolled over to reach for it.

No, don't, was her instinctive reaction.

But his hand had already swept the receiver up to his ear.

'Yes?' he said rather abruptly.

Sarah clutched the sheet up over her breasts as she sat up, pushing her hair back off her face at the same time. Who on earth could it be?

Not Chloe, she hoped, trying to worm her way back into Nick's life with a million apologies.

'For how long?' Nick asked in concerned tones. 'How bad are they?'

She had no idea whom he was talking to or what it was about. But it didn't sound like Chloe.

'No, I think you're right, Jim. Don't listen to her. She has to go to hospital. *Now*.'

Sarah sucked in sharply. Something was wrong with Flora!

'I don't think we should wait for an ambulance,' Nick told Jim quite firmly. 'Get her into the back of the Rolls and I'll drive you straight to St Vincent's. I'll just throw some clothes on.'

Slamming down the phone, he tossed back the sheet and jumped up.

'Flora's having chest pains,' he threw over his shoulder as he strode across the floor towards his walk-in wardrobe. 'I'm taking her to the hospital.'

'Can I come too?' Sarah asked, her heart racing with alarm.

'No, it'll take you too long to dress,' he said as he returned to the bedroom, jeans already on, a blue striped shirt in his hands.

'But I—'

'Let's not argue about this, Sarah.' He shoved his arms into the shirt's sleeves and drew it up over his shoulders. 'I'll call you from the hospital.'

'You haven't got any shoes on,' she pointed out when he headed for the door, shirt flapping open. 'You can't go to a hospital without shoes!'

He grumblingly went back for some trainers, then flew out of the door. Sarah heard him running down the stairs. Then she heard nothing.

A shiver ran down her spine, nausea swirling in her stomach at the possibility that Flora could be having a heart attack. She might even die!

The thought brought back all those horrible feelings she'd had when her father had been struck down by a coronary. Aside from the emotional trauma of losing her last parent, she'd been besieged with regret that she hadn't even been able to say goodbye to him, or tell him that she loved him.

Flora might not be a parent but Sarah loved her dearly. It pained her that Nick hadn't let her go with him, even though he was probably right—she would have taken longer to dress than him. He'd taken all of thirty seconds!

But that doesn't stop you from dressing now and following him to the hospital in your own car, does it?

Sarah was out of the bed in a flash, dashing for her room.

She didn't dress as fast as Nick, but she managed to make herself respectable in under ten minutes. Getting out of the house, however, took her another few minutes, because she had to lock up. Then she had difficulty finding the hospital, not having been there since her mother fell ill all those years ago. At last she located the right street, along with a parking spot not far from the emergency section.

She'd just made it to the ER waiting room when her mobile rang.

It had to be Nick, she reasoned as she retrieved it from her handbag.

'Nick?' she answered straight away.

'Where in hell are you?' he grumbled down the line. 'I tried the home number and you didn't answer.'

'I couldn't just sit there, Nick. So I got dressed and drove myself to the hospital. I've just arrived at the emergency waiting room. How's Flora?'

'Not too bad. They whipped her in and gave her some medication to thin her blood straight away. Then they hooked her up to some kind of heart-monitoring machine that does ECGs and other things. The doctor thinks it might just be angina.'

'But that's still not good, is it? I mean, angina can lead to a heart attack.'

'It can. But at least we've got her where she can have some further tests, and proper treatment. You know Flora. She doesn't like going to doctors, or hospitals. I'm going to make sure she stays in for a couple of days till we get a full picture of her condition. I've rung a colleague whose uncle is a top cardiac specialist here. We're going to transfer her to a private room after the doctor in ER is finished with her, and he'll come in in the morning and take over.'

Sarah felt the tension begin to drain out of her. 'That's wonderful, Nick. How's Jim doing?'

'To be honest, I've never seen him so distressed,' Nick whispered. 'He's sitting by Flora's bed as white as a sheet himself. I'm going to try to persuade him to come with me for a cup of tea and a piece of cake. I think he's in shock. Look, just sit down where you are and I'll be with you shortly. Then we can all go together. There has to be a cafeteria somewhere in here.'

'Couldn't I see Flora myself before we do that? I need to see her, Nick.' To tell her old friend that she loved her. Also that she was coming home to live. Permanently. She would put in for a transfer to a nearer school. No, she'd resign and find work in one of the many local preschools. They were always crying out for experienced infant teachers.

'She's not going to die, Sarah,' Nick said gently.

'You don't know that. What if she took a bad turn while I was sitting near by, having a cup of tea? I'd never forgive myself.'

'Fine. Stay where you are and I'll come and get you. I'll just tell Jim where I'm going.'

Sarah sat down in an empty chair against the wall, only then absorbing her surroundings. The place was very busy, with people rushing to and fro, and lots of people just sitting and waiting to be treated, several of them dishevelled young men with cuts and bruises over their faces. There were half a dozen mothers with crying children, and wailing babies. They all looked poor and wretched. Some of them even smelt.

She dropped her eyes away, upset by this brutal confrontation with the cold, cruel world. Not that she hadn't come across neglected children before. Just not on Christmas Day.

'Sarah? You OK?'

Sarah jumped up from the plastic chair. 'Oh, Nick, I'm so glad you're here.' She grabbed his arm and steered him away to one side.

'Did any of those louts bother you?' he asked.

'No, no, nothing like that. I just…Oh, Nick, the world's a horrible place, isn't it?'

'It can be,' he agreed soberly.

'We are so lucky to be healthy. And rich.'

His smile was wry. 'You're right there, sweetheart. Healthy and wealthy are the daily double. Come on, I'll take you to Flora.'

The sight of Flora's dull eyes and pale face alarmed Sarah. But she tried not to show it. 'What a scare you gave us,' she said lightly as she bent and kissed Flora on the cheek.

'It's just indigestion,' Flora protested. 'But no one believes me.'

The attending nurse surreptitiously rolled her eyes at Sarah, indicating that it certainly wasn't indigestion.

Sarah pulled up a chair by Flora's bed and picked up her hand. It felt oddly cold, which was another worry.

'Best we make sure, now that you're here,' she said.

Flora pressed her lips together. 'That's what Nick and Jim say but, truly, I'd much rather go home to my own bed. All I need is a rest.'

'Now, Flora, love,' an ashen-faced Jim began before his voice trailed weakly away. He'd never worn the trousers in the family and it looked as if he wasn't about to now.

'You'll do as you're told, madam,' Nick intervened firmly. 'Now I'm taking Jim for a cuppa. Sarah's going to sit with you for a while.'

Sarah flashed him an admiring smile. Truly, Nick's command of this situation had been wonderful from the word go. He hadn't panicked, he'd acted decisively and quickly—and possibly saved Flora's life in the process.

'See you soon,' he said to her, then turned and shepherded Jim away.

Sarah's gaze followed him for a while before returning to Flora.

'Have you something to confess, missie?' Flora said softly, but in a very knowing fashion.

Sarah had no intention of letting herself

be railroaded into any admissions about Nick. She would not hear the end of it if she told Flora that she and Nick were having an affair.

'I just wanted to say I love you dearly, Flora, and I've been a selfish cow, staying away from home as much I have. Things are going to change from now on, I assure you. I'm going to get a job near by so that I can be there, in person, to make sure you take it much easier, as well as look after your diet. I've become a very good cook of low-fat meals this past year, and you, madam, need to lose a few pounds. If you must work, then you can help Jim in the garden. And you're going to start walking. *Every* morning.'

'Goodness, you're sounding just like Nick.'

'Who has your best interests at heart as well. So I don't want to hear any more nonsense about your coming home just yet. Nick has organised a specialist to come in tomorrow to do some tests and you're going to have them.'

'Heavens to Betsy, is this my sweet little Sarah talking?'

'No, it's your grown-up Sarah.'

'I can see that. And so does Nick. He couldn't take his eyes off you today, Sarah. Or tonight, for that matter.'

Sarah eyed Flora sternly. 'Don't start matchmaking, Flora. You and I both know Nick is not a marrying man.'

'If anyone could make him change his mind about that, it's you, love.'

Sarah bit her tongue, lest she give the game away. But there was a part of her that agreed with Flora.

Nick hadn't just 'had sex' with her tonight. He'd made love to her, with tenderness and caring.

Who knew? Maybe there was a chance of a real relationship between them, no matter what Nick said.

'You're in love with him, aren't you?' Flora said.

Sarah could not bring herself to lie any longer. 'Yes,' she admitted.

'Then go after him, girl.'

'That's what I am doing.'

'And?'

Sarah felt a betraying smile tug at her lips. 'Let's just say it's a work in progress.'

'Ooooh, I like the sound of that.'

'Well, I don't,' the nurse interrupted firmly. 'Your blood pressure is on the rise again. Sorry,' she said to Sarah. 'I think it would be better if my patient rests quietly for a while. Perhaps you could join her other visitors in the coffee lounge for the next half-hour at least. It's thatta way.'

Sarah went reluctantly, with the solemn promise to return. She followed the direction of the nurse's finger, but still had to ask for more directions before she found the cafeteria.

Jim and Nick glanced up with questioning eyes at her arrival, Jim looking particularly anxious. She didn't have the heart to tell him that she'd raised his wife's blood pressure, saying instead that the nurse wanted Flora to rest quietly and they weren't to go back to her bedside for half an hour at least.

'If you want anything, you have to order at the counter,' Nick informed her.

Sarah shook her head. 'I don't want anything.'

'Don't be silly. I'll get you some coffee

and cake. You have to be hungry. I know I was.'

Jim said nothing during the time it took Nick to return with the coffee and piece of carrot cake. He just kept staring blankly into space.

'You haven't eaten your cake, Jim,' Nick said as he sat back down.

Jim turned his head towards Nick, his eyes remaining vacant. 'What did you say?'

'Your cake,' Nick said, nodding towards the untouched plate.

He shook his head. 'I can't eat it.'

'She's not going to die, Jim.'

'But what if she does?' he said plaintively. 'I can't live without her. She's all I have.'

'I know, Jim.' Sarah reached over to press a gentle hand on his arm. 'But you won't have to live without her. Not yet, anyway. We've caught this in time. We'll look after her together and make her better.'

His eyes filled with tears, shocking Sarah. She'd only ever seen a man cry once before in her life—her father, at her mother's funeral. Jim's crying propelled her back there, to her mother's graveside and the awful sound of her father's broken sobs as they lowered her coffin into the ground.

'I'm just so worried,' Jim choked out.

'We all are, Jim,' Nick said gently.

'I never thought I'd get married, you know,' Jim went on, his voice cracking some more. 'At forty, I was a crusty old bachelor. Not ugly exactly, but not the kind of chap women went for. Flora used to shop in the same supermarket as I did. Not sure why she took a liking to me but she did. Before I knew it, we were hitched.'

A huge lump filled Sarah's throat as she watched the tears run down Jim's sun-weathered cheeks.

'Best thing I ever did,' he finished up, pulling a hankie from his pocket.

An emotion-charged silence descended on their table. They all fell to drinking and eating, no one saying a word. Sarah noted that the people at the other tables weren't saying much either.

Cafeterias in hospitals, she decided, were not places of joy, especially late at night.

When her eyes returned to their table, she found Nick staring at her.

What are you thinking? she longed to ask.

But she said nothing, her eyes dropping back to her coffee.

Nick could not believe the crazy thoughts going through his head at that moment. Jim's touching little story about his romance with Flora must have totally unhinged him. Because, suddenly, he was thinking that that was what *he* should do: get married...to Sarah.

An incredibly bad idea. Even worse than giving in to his lust and sleeping with her. An affair with a scoundrel could have the beneficial side-effect of educating and protecting her, in a perverse kind of way. But marriage to the same scoundrel had nothing going for Sarah at all. Because such a union would not give her the one thing she wanted most in life: children.

This last thought steeled Nick's strangely wobbly heart, reaffirming his resolve to keep their affair strictly sexual. That way, when it was over, Sarah wouldn't be too hurt.

Meanwhile, it would be kinder of him if their affair didn't last too long. Best it be over by the time she turned twenty-five. Which gave him what time with her?

Six short weeks. Not long to burn out a lust that had been growing for years, and which he now had little control over. Despite all that had happened tonight, he could not wait to get her home, to bed. Which underlined just what type of man he was; not fit to marry a lovely girl like Sarah, that was for sure.

'I think we should go back to the ward now. See what they've discovered.'

Nick's abrupt suggestion jerked Sarah back to the moment at hand.

'The nurse didn't seem keen on Flora having too many visitors,' she told him. 'I think it would be best if I went home to bed. I'll come back and visit Flora tomorrow morning, bring her some things she might need.'

'That sounds like a good idea,' Nick agreed.

'I'm not going home,' Jim said somewhat stubbornly. 'I'm going to stay with my wife. They said I could.'

'Of course,' Nick soothed. 'I'll stay till I find out the doctor's verdict, then I'll go home too. I'll come back with Sarah in the morning.'

Nick stood up first, coming round to hold the back of Sarah's chair as she rose.

'*My* bed,' he whispered. 'Not yours.'

Shock held her rigid. How could he possibly be thinking about sex at this moment? It was the last thing on her mind.

But by the time she unlocked the front door and made her way upstairs, the thought of being with Nick again was slowly corrupting her. She kept telling herself that she was as wicked as he was; that she should be consumed with worry for Flora, not desire for him.

Nick's brief phone call from the hospital informing her that it had just been angina, and not a heart attack, did soothe her conscience somewhat, though her emotions were still very mixed as she showered and perfumed her body, then slipped, naked, back between those black satin sheets.

She'd heard about people having wildly tasteless sex at wakes, just to prove that they were still alive. Maybe this was something like that.

But she suspected not.

Sarah wanted to believe that it was love behind her behaviour. But she was beginning to wonder if it was more a matter of lust. She'd never experienced the kind of sexual pleasure that she'd had earlier that evening. And she wanted more.

By the time she heard the Rolls throttle down in the driveway, Sarah was beside herself with excitement. When Nick strode into the room already stripping off as he went, desire had rendered her totally mindless.

This time he did not speak and neither did she. Their coupling was fast and furious, a raw, animalistic mating that sent them both hurtling over the edge in seconds. Afterwards, they clung to each other, their skin pearled in sweat, their bodies stuck together.

'I didn't use a condom,' he muttered into her hair.

'I know,' she rasped.

'I'm sorry.'

'Don't be,' she shocked herself by saying. 'I liked it.'

Oh, what an understatement. She'd gloried in his hard, unprotected flesh surging into hers, wallowed in his flooding her womb.

His head lifted, dark eyes gleaming. 'But you're not safe. You've just opened the dungeon door, Sarah, big time.'

Her sex-glazed eyes searched his. 'What dungeon is that?'

'The one I've kept my X-rated fantasies about you imprisoned in all these years.'

Sarah's eyes widened at the rather menacing metaphor.

'Don't ever imagine I'm in love with you,' he snarled. 'Love doesn't live in a dungeon. Now, go to sleep. I've had enough for one night and I'm bloody exhausted.'

CHAPTER THIRTEEN

'SOMETHING to drink, Sarah?'

Sarah's head turned. She'd been staring through the plane window at the panoramic vista below. They'd not long taken off from Mascot Airport and hadn't yet reached any clouds.

'Yes, please,' she said to both Nick and the hovering stewardess. 'What can I have?'

'How about a glass of champagne?' Nick suggested.

'At seven-fifteen in the morning?'

'Why not?'

'Nick, you *are* terrible,' she chided, but jokingly. 'OK, champagne it is.'

'And you, sir?' the flight attendant asked.

'I'll have what she's having.'

Sarah's laugh enchanted him, as did she.

There was no artifice in her, no pretend sophistication. She was a pleasant change from the kind of woman he usually dated.

Once she was handed her glass of champagne, Sarah turned back to gaze intently through the window, her nose close to the rim.

Truly, she was like a child on her first flight.

Nick stared at her as he waited for his drink. She looked about sixteen this morning, wearing little make-up, no jewellery and a simple black and white sun-dress. Her hairstyle was young too, the sides scooped up into schoolgirlish combs, the rest falling loosely down her back.

The flight attendant was probably thinking he was a shameless cradle-snatcher. Nick detected a knowing glint in the woman's eyes as she handed him his glass of champagne.

Not that he cared what she thought, or anyone else for that matter. Nick had become so besotted by Sarah that he was already considering extending the length of their affair.

Of course, a month of non-stop sex with her at his holiday house on Happy Island might return him to a wiser course of action. He really hadn't had enough time to burn out his lust for Sarah since the first night they'd spent together.

Apart from anything, they'd been very busy, visiting Flora at the hospital and seeing to her health needs.

Fortunately, the specialist had located the source of the angina, a minor blockage in one artery that had been successfully cleared without the need for open-heart surgery. When the doctor had suggested a holiday for his quickly recovering patient, Nick had offered Jim and Flora his penthouse on the Gold Coast, which was fully serviced, with meals readily available, either in the restaurant downstairs or delivered to their apartment door. They'd jumped at the chance of an all-expenses-paid jaunt and Nick had seen them off at the airport three days ago, New Year's Eve.

Which had left him alone in the house with Sarah.

As Nick settled back to sip his champagne, his mind drifted back to the thirty-first of December…

He'd chilled some white wine, ordered in a five-star meal from a local restaurant, then set everything up on the balcony to the master bedroom, the perfect setting for a romantic, candlelit dinner. The perfect setting for New Year's Eve as well, with the uninterrupted view of Sydney Harbour—the water, the city and the bridge—which was always the showpiece of the fireworks.

Not that they got to see the fireworks, either at nine or at midnight, each occasion finding them otherwise occupied inside. After nearly a week of abstinence, he was insatiable, both for Sarah's beautiful body and her rapturous responses, Nick wallowing with wicked selfishness in the transparency of her feelings for him.

Nick could not get enough of her that night. Or the next day. Oddly enough, he didn't want to try out lots of different positions. He was content to just be in bed with her.

That evening, however, she suddenly called a halt, claiming she was exhausted. That night she slept alone, in her pink-quilted, little-girl bed.

Nick didn't argue. He could see she was determined. But he wasn't happy, resolving during that long, restless night that the following morning he would persuade her to go away with him to Happy Island, where she wouldn't be able to escape him.

Fortunately, he hadn't cancelled the airline tickets he'd booked for himself and Chloe.

Sarah's reaction to his invitation over breakfast seriously surprised Nick.

'Surely you can't expect me to go away with you on the same holiday you planned with Chloe!' she threw at him.

Nick quickly saw that his sensitivity meter was registering very low, Sarah making it clear what she thought of his suggestion.

He had to work hard all day to make Sarah see he wasn't treating her as a substitute for Chloe. Some tender lovemaking seemed to soften her stubborn attitude a little. But he finally struck the right note when he said that he'd never taken Chloe—or any of his other girlfriends—to Happy Island before. She would be the first female to share his holiday house with him.

It was both the truth, and a lie. He had

taken Chloe there for one short weekend back in September. But, as it had turned out, she'd fallen ill with food poisoning on the flight there. She'd been unwell the whole time, unable to do anything but stay in bed and read. Nick decided in his male mind that that didn't count.

After agreeing to go with him, Sarah had surprised him once again when she'd insisted on spending last night alone in her bedroom. She'd said she needed a good night's sleep, since they had to get up so very, very early.

Nick had been wide awake well before his alarm went off, his desire more intense than ever.

But it wouldn't be long now. Soon he would have her all to himself again in a place where she had nowhere to run to. Or to hide.

'Oh, I can't see anything any more,' Sarah said wistfully as she slumped back into her seat, her champagne glass still untouched. 'The clouds are in the way.'

Nick smiled. 'Anybody would think you hadn't flown before.'

'It's been years since I have,' she said, then finally took a sip of champagne.

'Really?'

'I haven't had much money left for holidays, what with paying for my rent and my car and general living expenses.'

Nick frowned. 'You could have asked me for some money for a holiday,' he said. 'I never did agree with Ray for leaving you that short of funds.'

'It was probably good for my character. At least I'm not spoiled.'

Nick's frown deepened. No, he thought. She certainly wasn't. But would spending time with him change her character? He wanted to educate her, not corrupt her. He would hate for her to turn out like Chloe, who thought of no one's pleasure but her own.

'Now, what's that frown all about?' she asked him. 'You're not worrying about Flora and Jim, are you? I spoke to them last night and they're as happy as can be up there on the Gold Coast. It was a brilliant idea of yours to lend them your penthouse. Very generous, too.'

Nick decided not to let her go back into hero-worship mode. Bad enough that she probably thought she was in love with him.

'Come, now, Sarah, you know very well it wasn't generosity that inspired my offer. It was a strictly selfish proposition. I wanted them right out of the way.'

'You're not the only one,' she said, then blushed.

It got to him, that blush, sparking a desire so intense that his flesh ached.

'I wish I could kiss you right now,' he said.

'Why can't you?' she returned, her cheeks still pink.

'Because I wouldn't want to stop there,' he ground out. 'Next thing you knew, we'd be joining the mile-high club.'

Her nose wrinkled with distaste. 'No way could you get me to do that. I've always thought sex on a plane to be the height of tackiness.'

'Hear! Hear!' Nick said, and raised his glass to her. No way, he realised with considerable relief, would she ever become like Chloe.

It would be damned difficult to go back to girls like Chloe after being with Sarah…

* * *

As Sarah sipped her champagne, she wondered if Nick really approved of her view. Maybe he thought her prudish, since he'd always claimed to be a roué.

But surprisingly, other than that first incident, when he'd pushed her down to her knees, her sexual encounters with him had not been the least bit decadent. Passionate, yes. But not dark.

On New Year's Eve he'd been very romantic, something he'd claimed he would never be.

Sarah held the opinion that people were as good, or as bad, as you let them be. Certainly, that applied to children. She'd discovered during her teaching years so far that if she had high expectations of her pupils they usually lived up to them.

Especially the so-called bad boys.

Nick was a bad boy. But he wasn't bad through and through, no matter what he thought of himself, and no matter what he'd done in the past. Her father had seen his worth. Her dad had also expected a lot of Nick. And Nick had lived up to those expectations.

Admittedly, he'd lost his way a bit since

Ray's death. Sarah could not deny that he had earned his playboy reputation. Women had been relegated to sex toys in his life for so long that it probably was foolish of her to think he would ever embrace a better way of life. With her.

Very foolish.

But love was foolish, wasn't it?

Why else was she sitting here, in a seat that had been booked for Chloe? The bottom line was that if Chloe hadn't made that *faux pas* on Christmas Day, she'd be the one sitting here today.

This pessimistic train of thought irritated Sarah to death. Hadn't she decided last night to be positive, and not negative; to view Nick's invitation to share a whole month with him as a step towards a real relationship? Hadn't she vowed to use this time not just to explore the sexual chemistry between them, but also to revive that special bond which had sprung up all those years ago when they'd both been so very lonely?

She hoped that, besides the sex, they would have deep and meaningful conversations during which Nick would tell her everything about himself, and vice versa.

'You're not drinking your champagne,' Nick pointed out.

Sarah turned a rueful smile his way. 'It *is* a little early. I think coffee would have been a better choice.'

'It's a woman's privilege to change her mind,' he said amiably, and pressed the button for service.

Sarah watched with pride as he gave the stewardess back the champagne and asked for coffee instead. She loved his decisiveness, his 'can-do' attitude. Nick was a natural leader, something her father had once commented on.

Sarah believed he would make a great husband and father. But would Nick ever believe it?

'I have a confession to make,' he said after the coffee arrived.

Sarah's stomach contracted. 'Nothing that will upset me, I hope.'

'No reason why it should.'

'Out with it, then.'

'I read all your Christmas cards. The ones on your dressing table.'

Her stomach relaxed. 'Oh? When?'

'Yesterday. When you were having a shower.'

'And?'

'I don't think I've ever seen such glowing words. It's a privilege to be in the company of the "bestest" teacher in the whole wide world.'

Sarah laughed. 'A slight exaggeration. But I am pretty good.'

'And yet you've resigned?'

'Only from my current school. I'll find another position closer to home. Possibly at a preschool. I'm very fond of small children. They have such open minds.'

'I don't have any patience with small children.'

'Lots of men don't. But they change, once they have their own.'

His glance was sharp. 'I won't. Because I don't intend having any of my own.'

Sarah kept her expression calm. 'Why's that?'

'Fathering is a learned skill, passed on from generation to generation. The only example I ever had of fathering is not something I'd like to pass on.'

'Not every child of abusive parents becomes an abuser themselves, Nick,' she said carefully.

'Perhaps not. But why take the chance? The world has enough children. They won't miss mine.'

'You might change your mind if you were presented with one.'

He whipped his head round to glare at her. 'You have brought your pills with you, haven't you? You're not going to try that old pregnancy trap. Because it won't work, Sarah. Not with me.'

The coldness in his eyes sent a chill running down her spine.

But she refused to give up on him. For now, anyway.

'I have no intention of trying to trap you with a baby, Nick. And yes, I have brought my pills. You can feed me one every day, if you'd like.'

'I just might do that.'

'Have you always been this paranoid about pregnancy?'

'Let's just say you're the first female I've ever had sex with without a condom.'

'It's nice to know that I'm unique.'

He smiled wryly as he shook his head at her. 'You are that, all right. Now, drink your coffee before it goes cold and I have to call the stewardess again.'

She drank her coffee quickly, anxious to get back to their conversation. It would be a couple more hours before they landed on Happy Island, with Nick imprisoned by her side all that time. Sarah didn't think she'd ever have a better opportunity to find out all the things she'd ever wanted to know about him. She suspected that once they hit Happy Island, there might not be too much talking done.

'Tell me about your life, Nick,' she said when she finally put the coffee down. 'Before you came to work for Dad. I'm curious.'

'I never talk about that part of my life, Sarah.'

'But that's silly. It's not as though I don't already know quite a bit. I know you had a horrible father and that you ran away from home to live on the streets when you were only thirteen. And I know that you were put in jail for car-stealing when you were eighteen.'

'Then you know enough, don't you?'

'Those are just the bare facts. I want you to fill in the details.'

Nick sighed. 'You do pick your moments.'

'I think I have the right to know some more about the man I'm sleeping with, don't you? You used to give my boyfriends the third degree.'

'But I'm not your boyfriend. I'm your secret lover. Secret lovers are often men of mystery.'

'Sorry, but you're not my secret lover any longer. I told Flora last night that we were together.'

'You *what*?'

Sarah shrugged. 'I said I was sorry.'

'Like hell you are. You're a conniving, manipulative little minx.'

Sarah could see that he wasn't as angry as he was trying to sound. And she had no intention of backing off.

'So are you going to tell me your life story, or not?'

'Do you think you're up for it, little girl?'

'Don't insult my intelligence, Nick. I might not have been around like you, but I watch the news at night, and I can read. I know about the big, bad world. Nothing you say will shock me.'

What a naïve statement, Sarah was to discover over the next quarter of an hour as she listened to Nick's dreadful life story.

His mother had run off when he'd been too young to remember her, his lone-parent father a violent and drunken good-for-nothing who taught his son to shoplift when he was only five and beat him every other day. Sarah was appalled as Nick described being not only punched and slapped, but also beaten with belts and burned with cigarettes.

Naturally, Nick's schooling had been limited—he was kept away a lot—but he was smart enough to learn to read and write. Love, of course, had been an unknown emotion. He'd counted himself lucky to be fed. Survival had been the name of the game.

When he'd gone into puberty at thirteen, he'd suddenly shot up in height and was able to look his father straight in the eye. For the first time when his father hit him, Nick had hit back.

He hadn't actually run away from home as she'd thought. He'd been literally thrown out into the street with only the clothes he was wearing.

He'd stayed in a refuge for a while, but was unfortunate enough to find one that was run by someone who wasn't interested in helping, just in pocketing his salary. Not the best introduction to the welfare system for an already emotionally scarred child. After running away from there, Nick had made his way to King's Cross in Sydney, where he squatted in derelict buildings and made money the only way he knew: by stealing. Not shoplifting. Mostly he broke into parked cars and stole the contents.

He'd resisted joining a gang, not wanting to rely on anyone but himself. He had made a few friends, but they were all low-life, pimps and prostitutes and drug-dealers. Inevitably, he'd been drawn into drug use himself. Anything to make his existence more bearable.

Addiction of any kind, however, took money. So he had started breaking and entering, plus stealing the cars themselves, rather than just the contents.

'One night,' he said, 'I made a mistake and got caught. I went to jail, met your father and the rest is history, as they say.'

Sarah was close to tears. 'Oh, Nick…'

'I did warn you.'

'You survived, though.'

'Let me tell you about that kind of survival,' he bit out. 'It makes you think of no one but yourself. You become hard, and cold, and capable of just about anything. When I first met your father when I was in jail, I didn't give a damn about him, only what he could do for me. I saw a means of escape and I grabbed it with both hands. When I finally got out of jail and came to work as Ray's chauffeur, I thought he was a sucker. I had no feelings for him whatsoever.'

'But you did, in the end,' she said. 'You *loved* him.'

'I respected him. That's not the same as love.'

'I see…'

'No, you don't. You don't see at all. You can't, till you've lived in my shoes. I've told you once, now I'll tell you again: men like me can't love anyone.'

'I don't believe that,' she muttered. She couldn't. For if she did, her future was unbearable. 'You weren't that bad when you came to live with us. You were kind to me for starters.'

'Was I? Or was I just trying to get in good with the boss?'

Sarah frowned. She'd never thought of his actions in that light before.

'Damn it all, don't look at me like that. OK, so I did like you. You were a nice kid.'

'You still like me,' she said with a smile of relief.

'Yeah. I still like you.'

As admissions went, it wasn't much, but it made Sarah feel better. Things suddenly looked a bit brighter. But she felt a change of subject was called for.

'Have you heard anything about your movie yet?'

She'd never seen Nick look so confused. *'What?'*

'Didn't you say that movie you'd put so much money into was coming out in the New Year? Well, it's the third of January. That's past the New Year.'

The penny dropped for Nick. His lurid background was too much for Sarah. Hopefully, she wouldn't bring it up again. Talking about movies he could cope with. His past was best kept locked in the dungeon.

'It came out yesterday to mixed reviews,' he told her. 'It'll take a few more days before the public's verdict has come in.'

'What's it called?'

'*Back to the Outback*. It's a sequel to *Outback Bride*. It has the same writer-director.'

'That should do well, surely. Everyone who saw and loved *Outback Bride* will come to see it.'

'That's what we're hoping.'

'Is it any good? Sequels often aren't as good as the original.'

'I think it is.'

'But the critics didn't.'

'A couple of them did. The others hated the tragic ending.'

'Who dies? Not Shane, I hope.'

'No, Brenda.'

'*Brenda!* That's even worse. You can't kill off the heroine in a romance. There has to be a happy ending, Nick.'

'Rubbish. Lots of romances have unhappy endings.'

'Only the ones written by men,' she said disgustedly. 'How does she die?'

'She's shot saving her child from the baddies,' he said defensively, as if that made it all right.

'No excuses. She simply cannot die. Why couldn't she have been shot, but still live? Truly, you should have talked to me about this earlier, Nick. I would have advised you.'

'She *needed* to die. She was no good for Shane. Their romance was flawed and their marriage was a disaster waiting to happen. She hated life in the country and was threatening to go back to the city and take the child when the baddies from her earlier life show up. The sequel isn't really a romance, Sarah, it's a drama.'

'You can call it what you like. It sounds awful.'

'Thank you for the vote of confidence.'

The captain announcing that they were expecting some turbulence and everyone was to belt up terminated what was becoming a heated exchange.

'Typical,' Nick muttered as he snapped his seat belt shut.

'What do you mean?' Sarah asked, grabbing at the armrests when the plane shuddered.

'January is cyclone season in this neck of the woods.'

'I wish you'd told me that earlier. We could have just as easily stayed home, especially once Flora and Jim went away.'

'I wanted to show you Happy Island.'

'The island itself, or your fancy holiday house?'

Nick smiled. 'A man's allowed to show off to his girlfriend, isn't he?'

Sarah's heart flipped over. 'You…you called me your girlfriend.'

Nick shrugged. 'I reserve the right to rescind the title if you get stroppy with me.'

'I only get stroppy during cyclones. I also get hysterical.'

Nick laughed. 'Now she tells me. Don't worry. My place is cyclone-proof. Actually, Happy Island hasn't been directly hit by a cyclone in decades. Mostly, it just gets lots of wind and rain. Unfortunately, we might have to stay indoors for days on end,' he added with a wicked twinkle in his eyes.

Sarah grinned. 'Just as well I brought all my old board games with me, then, isn't it?'

Nick groaned. 'Oh, no, not the Monopoly! You always whipped my butt at that.'

'Monopoly and Snakes and Ladders, and Chinese Checkers. I found them in the bottom of my wardrobe when I was packing.'

When Nick looked pained, she gave him a playful dig in the ribs.

'Come on. We used to have great fun playing those games.'

'I had some different kinds of games in mind now that you've grown up.'

Sarah shook her head at him. 'If you think this holiday is going to be just a sex-fest, Nick, then think again. I picked up a brochure about Happy Island from a local travel agent and there's heaps I want to do.'

'Really. Such as?'

'Aside from a tour around the island to all the scenic spots, I'd like to take a boat trip to the barrier reef and a helicopter ride over the Whitsundays. Then there's windsurfing and souvenir-shopping. Oh, and mini-golf. You can have your revenge on me with that. I also saw pictures of a lovely white beach with the most beautiful turquoise waters where I'd like to go for a swim.'

'Uh-uh,' he said with a shake of his head. 'You won't be doing that.'

'Why not?'

'Because of the irukanji.'

'The what?'

'They're a jellyfish. Toxic as all hell. They can put you in hospital for days. Two people have died from their sting since 2001. Summer is their peak season.'

'Oh, great. No swimming.'

'Actually, you *can* go in the sea, if you

wear a full body suit. But they don't look too glamorous. Still, not to worry. There are more swimming pools on Happy Island than you can poke a stick at. Mine is fabulous, and solar-heated as well.'

'I didn't doubt it.'

His smile carried amusement. 'You have a tongue on you at times, don't you?'

'I never said I was perfect.'

'Just nearly,' he murmured, and leant over to kiss her on the cheek.

Her head turned fully to face him. 'I thought you said you weren't going to kiss me.'

'You call that a kiss? I'll show you a kiss when I get you to my place.'

A quiver ran through her body at the desire gleaming bright in his eyes. This was what she'd always wanted, to have him look at her like this. But would it be enough, just being the recipient of Nick's passion? The truth was she wanted more now. She wanted that happily-ever-after ending. She wanted Nick's love, the very thing he claimed he could never give anyone.

'You can relax your hands now,' he said. 'We're through the turbulence.'

Not so, she thought with a tormented twist to her heart. The turbulence has only just begun.

CHAPTER FOURTEEN

THE beauty of Happy Island just blew Sarah away. The pilot circled it once before landing, giving all the window-seat passengers a splendid view.

Talk about a tropical paradise!

She'd heard people wax lyrical about the colour of the sand and the water in this region, but the beaches and bays were just magic to the eye, framed by lots of palm trees and environmentally friendly buildings that blended beautifully with the green vegetation.

Nick was right about the number of pools, though. They did stand out from the air, because there were so many, in all sorts of shapes and sizes.

Any worry she was still harbouring about the eventual outcome of their relationship was put aside as excitement took hold. It would be wonderful to have a romantic holiday here, with the man she loved. Wonderful to have him all to herself for a whole month.

If nothing else, she would have this marvellous memory.

'No point in rushing off the plane,' Nick said when everyone else jumped up from their seats. 'We'll only have to wait in the heat for our luggage. There's no carousel in the terminal here, just a collection area down near where all the resort shuttles are parked.'

'Will we be taking a shuttle?'

'No. I own a golf buggy, which I keep at the airport.'

'Oh, yes, I read about those in the brochure. It said there weren't many cars on the island, and everyone got around in golf buggies.'

'That's right.'

'Can I drive it?'

'Sure.'

'Oh, wow. That'll be fun.'

Sarah and Nick finally exited the plane next to last, with Sarah surprised to find it not quite as hot outside as she'd been expecting. 'Am I wrong, or is it not all that hot out here?'

'No, you're quite right. But the weather forecast says there'll be a change later in the week. It's going to gradually get hotter, with higher temperatures and humidity. They're predicting a storm on Saturday afternoon, with strong gusts of wind and tons of rain.'

'How do you know all that?'

'Looked on the internet last night for the forecast up this way.'

'You didn't bring your laptop with you, I hope.'

'No need. I have a full computer set-up here.'

'What *don't* you have here?' Sarah heard herself saying half an hour later.

She was standing in the main living room of Nick's holiday house, looking through a wall made totally of glass at the most magnificent pool she had ever seen. It was called a horizon pool, so named because the far side of the pool seemed to have no edge, the water meeting the sky the way the horizon did out at sea.

'It cost me a pretty penny,' Nick agreed.

'You mean the pool, or the rest of this place?'

Actually, the house wasn't all that huge. Only three bedrooms. But everything was beautifully and stylishly decorated in cool greens and blues that complemented its tropical setting. There was also every mod con available, including a kitchen to die for and a king-sized plasma television.

'The foundations cost the most,' he told her.

Sarah could understand why. The house was built on the side of a cliff, its half-hexagonal shape creating one-hundred-and-eighty-degree views. All the rooms had huge glass windows or walls that looked out to sea and the other islands beyond. The glass was specially toughened to withstand even the worst storms, Nick told her, and tinted to soften any glare.

'It took two years to build,' Nick said. 'It was only completed last June.'

'Really?' Sarah said. So that was why Nick hadn't brought any of his girlfriends here before. He hadn't had the opportunity. Still, it was nice to think she was the first girl to stand here with him. And the first to share this particular master bedroom. She could hardly make the same claim about the bedroom back home.

'It's spectacular, Nick,' she said, throwing a warm smile up at him. 'So's this view.'

Nick slid an arm around her waist and pulled her close. 'Wait till you see it at sunrise.'

When he turned her towards him, Sarah knew he was going to kiss her. And this time, there would be no stopping him. Not that she wanted to. Her heart was already pounding by the time his lips met hers.

'I don't think I'm going to let you unpack,' Nick said to her some considerable time later. 'I like you like this.'

They'd eventually made it to the master bedroom, though Sarah's clothes were still on the living-room floor. Nick's as well.

Sarah sighed with pleasure as Nick gently caressed her stomach.

'I like you like this as well,' she returned dreamily.

The lovemaking between them was getting better and better, and gradually more adventurous. Sarah had thought she preferred the missionary position with Nick, where their eyes could meet and she could hold him close in the traditional way. But she found this spoon position very much to her liking, thrilling to the hot feel of Nick's body cocooned around hers. She loved that it left his hands free to play with her breasts and the rest of her body whilst he was inside her. The sensations had sent her head spinning.

He hadn't withdrawn afterwards, and she could feel him slowly coming back to life. He groaned when her bottom moved voluptuously against him.

His hands lifted to her breasts, where he pinched her nipples.

'Oh,' she gasped, startled by the odd mixture of pain and pleasure.

'You liked that,' he muttered thickly in her ear.

'Yes…no…I don't know.'

'*I* liked it,' he said, and did it again.

She moaned, then squirmed. Yes, she definitely did like it.

'Do it again,' she urged breathlessly.

He obliged and her head whirled with the

dizziest pleasure. Now he was fully erect again, and began thrusting harder than the first time. Heat enveloped her, her forehead breaking into a sweat.

'Yes,' she bit out, everything inside her twisting into exquisitely expectant spirals. 'Yes. Yes,' she cried out as her body broke into little pieces, splintering apart with a violent release.

With a raw groan Nick rolled her over onto her stomach, cupping her breasts and lifting her up onto her hands and knees. Sarah thought she was done, but she was wrong. When he reached down and rubbed her clitoris, another orgasm ripped through her. This time he came too, hot and strong. At last she fell, face-down, onto the bed, his body collapsing on top of hers.

For a couple of minutes they just lay, glued together by sweat, their breathing ragged.

'See?' he said at last, his voice low and thick. 'A woman can come lots of times in a row. I could keep you coming all day, if you want me to.'

Sarah went weak with the thought of his doing such a thing.

'I...I think what I need right at this moment,' she said shakily, 'is a shower.'

'Mmm. What a good idea. I'll join you.'

CHAPTER FIFTEEN

NICK lay stretched out next to Sarah's sleeping form, his hands linked behind his head, his body temporarily sated but his mind not even remotely at peace.

It wasn't working, his plan to burn out his lust for Sarah. It seemed the more he had her, the more he wanted her.

Thirty-six hours had passed since their arrival, with their hardly leaving the master suite, except for food and the occasional dip in the pool.

Nick's flesh began to stir once more as he recalled their erotic encounter by the pool last night, not to mention the wildly passionate one in the kitchen this morning.

Sarah had confessed afterwards she'd never had sex whilst sitting on a granite bench-top before. Or sitting anywhere, for that matter.

It seemed her sex life so far had been limited and unimaginative, a fact that Nick found surprising, yet primally satisfying. He was beginning to understand why some men married virgins. There had to be something intensely pleasing about being a female's first lover.

At the same time, Sarah's lack of sexual experience troubled him. Young, naïve girls like her fell in love so very easily.

Though she'd never said she loved him, he'd seen adoration in her lovely but very readable eyes. Seen it, and wallowed in it.

Was that the reason behind his growing addiction for her? Not the sex so much but the way Sarah made him feel whilst he was making love to her?

How would it be to always have her in his bed? he began to wonder. To put his ring on her finger? To legally bind her to him?

Crazy thoughts, Nick. Crazy.

Shaking his head, he rolled over and propped himself up on one elbow to stare down at her, his eyes roving hotly over her lusciously naked body. Before he knew it he was touching her again, waking her, *wanting* her. He groaned when she opened her arms to him on a sigh of sweet surrender.

Say no, damn you, his mind screamed as he plunged into her.

But she didn't.

Sarah crept from the bed, lest she wake Nick. Night had fallen and he was sleeping soundly at long last.

Pulling on her lavender satin robe—her only item of clothing as yet unpacked—she made her way quietly out to the kitchen, where she began to search the large freezer for something substantial to eat. During the past two days they'd only eaten enough to survive—mostly toast and coffee—and Sarah was suddenly feeling ravenous.

Half an hour and two microwaveable meals later, Sarah carried a second mug of coffee into the living room and curled herself up in a corner of the blue sofa. She sighed as she sipped, only then allowing herself to think about what they'd been doing since they'd arrived on Happy Island.

So much for her saying this holiday was not going to be just a sex-fest!

Truly, she should put her foot down and demand that they leave the house occasionally. It wasn't right to just loll around, having sex all the time.

Sarah pulled a face. Maybe it wasn't right, but it felt good. *She* felt good. Better than she'd ever felt.

But enough was enough, she decided. Come tomorrow, she would insist on their getting dressed and going out somewhere.

Hopefully Nick would not make a fuss, or start seducing her again. Her head whirled at how good he was at doing that. And how successful. She just couldn't seem to say no to him.

But she would, come tomorrow morning.

Easier said than done, Sarah thought ruefully. He only had to roll over and start touching her, and she was a goner.

Maybe she should spend the rest of the night out here on this sofa; it was big enough to sleep on.

Whatever, she didn't need sleep for a while. After her eating binge, she was wide awake. Watching television was not an option, however. The noise might wake Nick. Maybe she would read for a while. There were a few paperbacks on the shelves that flanked the large built-in entertainment unit.

Sarah put down her coffee and made her way across the tiled floor. There was only one title that appealed, called *Dressed to Kill*, the back blurb promising a page-turning thriller with twists and turns and a spine-tingling climax.

Sarah's spine certainly tingled when she opened it and saw the handwritten name on top of the first page.

Chloe Cameron.

Her mouth went dry as she stared down at that hated name, her head filling with a hundred horrible thoughts, the main one being that Nick had lied to her. Chloe *had* been to Happy Island with him—how else would this book be here? Nick was not a reader.

Various repulsive images popped into Sarah's mind. Of Nick having sex with Chloe by the pool and on the kitchen counter. Of his doing all the things with Chloe that he'd done with her.

The hurt was overwhelming. So was the humiliation. What a fool she'd been to be so easily tricked! A besotted fool!

But no more.

Gripping the book tightly in both hands, Sarah marched back into the bedroom, snapping on the overhead light, then slamming the door with deliberate loudness.

Nick woke with a start, blinking madly as he sat up. Sarah's glowering at him from the side of the bed brought confusion, then a jolt of alarm.

'What is it? What's wrong?'

She threw something at him. A book. It struck his bare chest before he could catch it, tumbling down into his lap.

'You said you'd never brought her here,' Sarah bit out. 'You lied, you bastard.'

The penny dropped for Nick, as did his stomach.

'It's not what you're thinking,' he defended.

Her laugh had a hard, hollow sound to it. 'And why's that, Nick?'

'I didn't have sex with her.'

She laughed again. 'You expect me to believe that? Mr I-have-to-have-it-ten-times-a-day!'

'Chloe was sick, with food poisoning. She spent the whole weekend in bed in the guest room.'

Sarah crossed her arms, her expression scornful. 'If that's the truth, why didn't you tell me?

'I'll tell you why,' she went on before he could say a single word. 'Because that might not have got you what you wanted, which was stupid me, filling in for Chloe on this holiday. Better to let the silly little fool think she's unique and special. Make her believe your inviting her to come with you here is a one-off. Whatever way you look at it, Nick, you lied to me for your own selfish ends.'

Nick was not at his best when backed into a corner. He always came out fighting.

'And you haven't done the same?' he counter-attacked. 'I seem to recall your telling me in my study on Christmas Day that all you wanted from me was sex. Obviously that wasn't the truth, was it? You want what you've always wanted: marriage. That's why you've been so damned accommodating all the time. And why you're so upset right now!'

Her face flushed with a shaming heat, her hurt eyes making him feel totally wretched.

'If that's what you really think, Nick,' she choked out, 'then I can't stay here with you. I just can't.'

In all his life, Nick had never felt so dreadful. Even when he'd been in jail. But it was for the best, wasn't it? He was no good for her. Better they call it quits now before she got even more hurt.

'If that's what you want,' he snapped.

'What I want…' She shook her head, her shoulders slumping as a soul-weary sigh escaped her lips. 'I'm never going to get what I want. Not with you. I can see that now.' She straightened, putting her shoulders back and lifting her chin up. 'I'm sorry for throwing that book at you, Nick. Generally speaking, you have been honest with me. Quite brutally at times. I just didn't want to hear what you were saying.'

Now Nick felt even worse, his heart like

a great lump of iron in his chest. The temptation to jump up and take her in his arms was almost overwhelming. He wanted to tell her that *he* was the sorry one, that she *was* unique and special and that he *did* want to marry her.

But he resisted the temptation. Somehow.

'I…I'll move my things into one of the spare bedrooms for tonight,' she went on, her eyes glistening. 'Then first thing tomorrow I'll see if I can get on a flight back to Sydney.'

'Fine,' he said, and threw back the sheet. 'Now, if you'll excuse me, I need to go to the bathroom.'

CHAPTER SIXTEEN

SARAH couldn't sleep. Not only was she still very upset, but she was also hot. The weather forecast had been right: the temperature had risen sharply over the last few hours, so the air-conditioning was struggling in the higher humidity.

In the end, Sarah got up, put on the pink bikini she'd bought before Christmas, grabbed a towel and headed for the pool. Who cared if it was the middle of the night and pitch-black outside? The pool had underwater lighting.

The strength of the wind surprised her. She had to anchor her towel underneath a banana lounger to stop it from blowing away. The same banana lounger, she realised, that she and Nick had had sex on the day before. Wild, wanton sex, with herself a very willing partner.

Shuddering at the memory, Sarah dived into the water, and began stroking vigorously up and down, hoping to make herself so exhausted that when she returned to bed she would immediately fall asleep.

Fat chance, she thought wretchedly, but continued to punish herself with lap after lap. Finally, the lactic acid in her joints forced her to stop. Slowly, she swam over towards the lounger that was down near the far edge of the pool.

Sarah shivered as she hauled herself out of the water. The wind was much stronger than before. That storm couldn't be far off now. Hopefully, it wouldn't last too long. She didn't want there to be any reason for the airport to be closed tomorrow. She needed to get off this island and away from Nick as soon as possible.

Sarah was bending to retrieve her towel when a wildly swirling gust of wind lifted a nearby table and umbrella off the tiled surrounds and hurled them against her back. She screamed as she was catapulted with tremendous force into the air and right over the horizon edge of the pool. She screamed again when she hit the water-catching ledge below with a bruising blow to her shoulder, another scream bursting from her mouth when momentum carried her right off the edge and into the void.

Nick was lying on top of the sheets, wide awake, when he heard Sarah's terrified screams. He was off the bed in a flash, fear quickening his heartbeat—and his legs—as he raced in the direction of her cries.

The pool area.

The security light was already on, indicating that Sarah must have come outside here recently. But he couldn't see her anywhere.

And then he saw them: the table and umbrella floating in the far end of the pool.

'Oh, my God!' he exclaimed, his first thought being that she was under them in the water, knocked unconscious and already drowning.

When Nick dived in and found no sign of her, an even worse possibility came to mind. Swimming to the far edge, he peered over it to the ledge below, hoping against hope that he'd see her sitting there, waiting for him to pull her up into his arms.

The most appalling dread consumed him when the dimly lit ledge proved empty as well. The thought that she had fallen down to the rocky waters below was so horrendous that he could hardly conceive of it. For no one could survive a fall like that.

'Nooooo!' he screamed into the wind.

She could not be dead. Not his Sarah. Not his wonderful, beautiful, sweet Sarah.

'Nick! Nick, are you there?'

Nick almost cried with relief. 'Yes, I'm here,' he called back, scrambling over the edge and dropping down to the ledge below. 'Where are you? I can't see you!'

His eyes were gradually becoming accustomed to the lack of direct light, but the wind was making them water like mad.

'Down here.'

'Down where?'

He leant right over as far as he dared, finally spotting her clinging to the cliff a few metres down under the ledge. No, not to the cliff but to a bush that was growing out of a crevice in the rock face—a rather straggly-looking bush.

Hopefully, the roots were tenacious.

'Have you got a foothold?' he called out to her.

'A bit of a one. But I think this bush is coming loose. Oh, God, yes, it is. Do something, Nick.'

Nick knew she was too far down for him to reach. He needed something long that she could get hold of. But what?

Panic turned his head to mush for a moment.

'Think, man,' he muttered to himself.

The umbrella in the pool. It was quite large and its supporting pole was long.

'Hold on, Sarah, I have an idea.'

Adrenaline had him leaping back up and into the pool with the agility of a monkey. He grabbed the umbrella, yanked it down, then jumped back with it to the ledge below.

'Here,' he said, and stretched it out towards her. 'Grab this.'

She did so.

'Hold on tight,' he ordered.

Her weight surprised him at first. But he felt strong, stronger than he'd ever felt. And then she was there, in his arms, weeping and shaking with shock.

Nick held her close, his lips buried in her wet hair, his eyes tightly shut.

'It's all right,' he said thickly. 'I have you now. You're safe.'

'Oh, Nick,' Sarah cried. 'I…I thought I was going to die.'

Nick held her even tighter. He'd thought she *had* died. And it was the most defining moment in his life. He knew now what Jim had felt at that hospital. Because as much as Jim loved Flora, *he* loved Sarah. Oh, yes, he loved her. There was no longer any doubt in his mind.

But did that make any difference? Wouldn't she still be better off if he let her go?

He just didn't know any more.

'I…I can't stop sh-shaking,' she said, her teeth chattering.

'You're in shock,' he told her. 'What you need is a warm bath, and a hot cup of tea with lots of sugar in it. But first, I have to get you up out of here. Very, very carefully.'

* * *

Sarah couldn't stop thinking about the moment she'd fallen off that ledge. Couldn't stop reliving the fear, and the split-second realisation that her life was about to be over.

It made one reassess things, facing death like that. Made one see what was important, and what wasn't. Made one more prepared to take a risk or two.

'Here's the tea,' Nick said as he came into the bathroom.

Sarah was lying back in a very deep, deliciously warm bath, her pink bikini still on. Nick, however, was still naked.

'Do you think you could put something on?' she said to him when he handed her the tea. Sarah knew she would find it difficult to talk to a naked Nick.

And she did want to talk to him. Sensibly and truthfully.

Nick pulled a towel off a nearby rail and tied it around his hips.

'This do?' he asked her.

'Yes, thank you. No, please don't leave. I…I have something I want to say to you.'

Nick crossed his arms and leant against the far wall whilst Sarah lifted the mug to her lips and swallowed, grimacing at the excessive sweetness. Finally, she put the mug down and locked eyes with him.

'I've decided I don't want to go home tomorrow.'

His eyes flickered momentarily. 'And why's that, Sarah?'

'I love you, Nick. I've always loved you. You were quite right about why I came here with you. I had this romantic dream that if we spent quality time together, you would discover that you loved me back. And then there was the ultimate fantasy of your asking me to marry you.'

Now he did move, his arms uncrossing as he levered himself away from the wall, his high forehead drawing into a frown. 'Sarah, I—'

'No, no, let me finish, please, Nick.'

'Very well.'

'You may have been right about my reasons for coming here with you. But you were wrong when you accused me of using sex to try to get what I wanted. Not once have I said yes to you sexually with that agenda in mind. I *love* it when you make love to me. I've never experienced anything like it before in my life. I can't describe how I feel when you're inside me. I don't want to walk away from that pleasure, Nick. So if you still want me, I'd like to stay. I...I promise I won't put on any more insanely jealous turns. I just want to be with you, Nick,' she finished, a huge lump having formed in her throat during her brave little speech. 'Please...I...'

When her eyes filled with tears, Nick couldn't stand it any longer. How could his sending her away be the best thing for her? Or him? Seeing her like this was killing him.

'Don't cry,' he choked out as he fell to his knees by the bath. 'Please don't cry.'

'I'm sorry,' she sobbed. 'It's just...I...I love you so much.'

His hands reached out to cup her lovely face. 'And I love you, my darling.'

She gasped, her eyes widening.

'I knew it tonight when I thought I'd lost you. I love you, Sarah. And I *do* want to marry you.'

Her eyes carried shock, and scepticism.

'You…you don't mean that. You can't. You always said…'

'I know what I always said. I thought I wasn't good enough for you.'

'Oh, Nick. That's just so not true.'

'Yes, it is,' he insisted. 'But if you will trust me with your life I vow that I will do my best never to hurt you, or let you or your father down. I will be faithful only to you. I will love you and protect you. And I will love and protect our children.'

Her already shocked eyes rounded further. 'You're prepared to have children?'

'I'll have your children, my darling, because I know that any shortcomings I have as a father will be more than made up for by your brilliance as a mother.'

'You…you shouldn't say such sweet things to me,' she cried.

'Why not? I mean them.'

Her tear-filled eyes searched his. 'You do mean them, don't you?'

'I surely do.'

'I…I don't know what to say.'

'Yes to marrying me would be a good start.'

'Oh, yes,' she said, and he kissed her.
When his mouth lifted she was smiling.

'I'm glad to see I was right,' she said.

'About what?' Nick asked.

'The heroine in a romance never dies.'

EPILOGUE

'DON'T you think people might think it's odd,' Flora said, 'having a sixty-one-year-old bridesmaid?'

'Who cares what people think?' Sarah countered. 'Besides, you look absolutely beautiful.' She did, too. A few weeks of healthy eating and exercising had done wonders. So did her new blonde hair. Flora looked ten years younger.

'Not as beautiful as the bride,' Flora returned with a warm smile. 'I'm so happy for you and Nick, love. If ever a couple were made for each other it's you two. Ray would have been very pleased. Pleased about the baby, too.'

'I think so,' Sarah said, beaming with happiness.

She'd forgotten to take the Pill the morning after that traumatic night on Happy Island, and had fallen pregnant. At first she'd been a bit nervous about Nick's reaction, but he'd been absolutely thrilled.

It seemed mother nature knew what she was doing.

Now here she was, almost four months pregnant, about to marry the father of her baby and the only man she'd ever loved. She was not, however, a super-rich heiress. The day before her twenty-fifth birthday, she'd discussed her feelings over her inheritance with Nick and decided to do what he'd once said her father should have done in the first place: give all the money to charity.

So she had, dividing up the many millions in the estate between various charities that supported the poor and the needy.

Of course, she wasn't exactly broke. She still owned Goldmine, which was worth a conservative twenty million. Not that she would ever sell it. And then there were the royalties from *Outback Bride*, which would continue to flow in, the movie having been re-released after the worldwide success of its sequel. Nick had been so right about that tear-jerker ending.

Generally speaking, however, Nick would be the main provider for their family, an excellent source of motivation for him to keep working hard and feeling good about himself. Sarah vowed to never forget that underneath her husband's façade of confidence lay a damaged child who constantly needed the healing power of love. *Her* love.

A loud knock on her bedroom door was accompanied by a familiar voice. 'Time for the bride to make an appearance downstairs. We don't want the groom thinking things, do we?'

Sarah was smiling as she opened the door.

'Wow!' Derek said, looking her up and down. 'It's at moments like these I wish I weren't gay. And I'm not just talking about the bride.'

'Oh, go on with you,' Flora said, but with a big grin on her face.

Derek had become a frequent visitor to Goldmine, with Nick even warming to him. Derek had been delighted—and touched—when Sarah had asked him to give her away.

'OK, girls,' he said, linking arms with Sarah, 'it's showtime!'

'Goddamn!' Jim exclaimed beside Nick when an elegantly dressed blonde lady walked sedately down the steps into the rather crowded family room. 'Is that my Flora?'

'Indeed it is,' Nick informed his best man. But his own admiring eyes moved quickly to the radiant bride following Flora, his heart filling with emotion as he watched Sarah walk towards him with the most glorious smile on her face. It was a smile of total love and trust, that love and trust which had soothed his soul and brought it out from the dungeon into the light.

Nick still found it hard to believe sometimes that he was happy about becoming a husband and father. Still, anything was possible with Sarah by his side.

'You look amazing,' he said softly to her as he took her hand and they turned to face the celebrant.

'You do, too,' she whispered back.

'Ray would have been so proud of you.'

Her hand squeezed his tightly. 'You, too, my darling heart. You, too.'

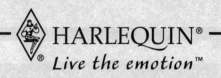

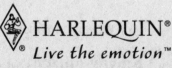

HARLEQUIN®
INTRIGUE®

BREATHTAKING ROMANTIC SUSPENSE

Shared dangers and passions lead to electrifying romance and heart-stopping suspense!

Every month, you'll meet six new heroes who are guaranteed to make your spine tingle and your pulse pound. With them you'll enter into the exciting world of Harlequin Intrigue— where your life is on the line and so is your heart!

THAT'S INTRIGUE—
ROMANTIC SUSPENSE
AT ITS BEST!

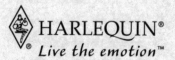

HARLEQUIN®
Live the emotion™

HARLEQUIN®
Presents

The world's bestselling romance series...
The series that brings you your favorite authors,
month after month:

Helen Bianchin...Emma Darcy
Lynne Graham...Penny Jordan
Miranda Lee...Sandra Marton
Anne Mather...Carole Mortimer
Susan Napier...Michelle Reid

and many more uniquely talented authors!

Wealthy, powerful, gorgeous men...
Women who have feelings just like your own...
The stories you love, set in exotic, glamorous locations...

HARLEQUIN®
Presents

Seduction and Passion Guaranteed!

HPDIR104

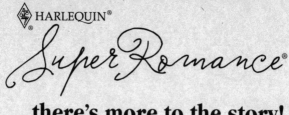

HARLEQUIN®
Super Romance®

...there's more to the story!

Superromance.
A *big* satisfying read about unforgettable
characters. Each month we offer *six* very different
stories that range from family drama to adventure
and mystery, from highly emotional stories to
romantic comedies—and much more! Stories
about people you'll believe in and care about.
Stories too compelling to put down....

Our authors are among today's *best* romance
writers. You'll find familiar names and talented
newcomers. Many of them are award winners—
and you'll see why!

If you want the biggest and best
in romance fiction, you'll get it
from Superromance!

Exciting, Emotional, Unexpected...

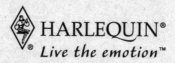

HARLEQUIN®
Live the emotion™